MISTER X

Patron saint of Murder

Contents

Foreword

Legends, fairy tales, and myths. Each is a type of story, each holds a form of truth. Stories can be portrayed in varying structures and styles, from music, to poetry, to pictures, and verbal and written narratives. Whether fiction or fact, stories hold power. They spark creativity and draw out emotion. An engaging story can provoke anger, love, passion, inspiration, curiosity, despair, and hope. Each story we compose shapes the world around us; history is a prime example of this. Stories have the power to change the world, but for better or worse is anyone's guess. Ladies and gentlemen, I am your humble storyteller, and today I have a tale to share with you. Hopefully, this story will change your perception of the world and the power of the stories that fabricate it. For all you know, this introduction alone has already changed your perspective. So, without further ado, let us begin.

Act I

Chapter I

I despise the holidays and always have. I never understood how people could find such merriment in "the most wonderful time of the year." Let's be honest, this annoying holiday is really just an excuse to extort gifts and time from the people you "care about" and to promote "peace on earth." It boggles the mind to see how much Christmas has evolved over the years. What started as a pagan holiday originating in Rome, where debauchery was a favorite pastime, is now a religious holiday invoking peace, togetherness, and holiness— whatever that's supposed to mean. I wonder how many years we have left before Christmas morphs into something unrecognizable once again. It's not my intention to be a Scrooge or to spoil anyone's rum and eggnog. It's just that I've always found the holidays boring and mundane. Most people would be content relaxing during this time, but my work tends to be put on hold for me. As you know it's the most peaceful time of the year. It's as if the criminal element itself took a holiday. Go figure.

Growing tired of the peaceful days, I spent my time casually throwing darts in my office.

"Bullseye," I muttered.

I took my stance and aimed to score another. Realizing I was out of darts, I snapped my fingers and the darts returned to my side once again. A yawn escaped my lips as I gathered them. Though this process sounds monotonous, I found it strangely cathartic. It was a good exercise to focus my mind. In addition to improving my aim, throwing darts also distracted me from the monotony of everyday life. Again, I took a dart, prepared my stance, and aimed at the empty board. Oh, how rude of me, I should introduce myself and what I actually—.

"Knock, knock," said a voice outside my door.

"Come in," I said, prepping my shot.

"We got mail!"

The sudden shout caused me to throw my dart prematurely and I missed my target by a few inches. I glared at the culprit despite his apologetic smile. Perhaps I should introduce him. My canine friend, who is as large as a Timber wolf and as loyal as a Kangal, is my partner, Zed. We've been together for years. We're in the same business so it was only natural that we live together.

"Sorry, didn't know you were busy," said Zed.

My annoyance subsided with a brief sigh.

"I'm *not* busy, that's why I'm playing," I explained as I snapped my fingers and returned the dart.

"Be careful not to overuse your *Grace*. You know how you can get when you do," Zed chided.

I yawned and Zed shook his head.

"Anyway, here's the mail." Zed presented a fistful of sealed envelopes.

"I am thankful for you getting the mail, Zed, but seriously, you don't have to give me the mail in that form," I said, relinquishing the mail from his snout.

I sifted through the letters, finding one bill after another, until I came across a peculiar notice. The letter, with a weathered exterior and a natural color with a yellowish tint, seemed ominous, so I looked closer to inspect the contents. The envelope wasn't stained, the yellow was just the hue of the paper. It was high-quality paper.

A weird design, even for this time of year, I thought.

On the front was a red wax seal engraved with a cross. I cracked the seal to reveal the contents within. It was a simple card sparse with words, but clear and direct.

"Naughty boys get a stocking full of coal."

The word naughty was emboldened in a dark red ink that looked very similar to oxidized blood. It gave me an eerie feeling. "Zed, come sniff this letter," I said. He looked at me in annoyance.

"Fine," he said with a long, drawn-out sniff. "It's scentless," he said.

"Weird. Even ink tends to have a smell. This must be some substitute," I said.

I looked at the envelope one last time and found an address on the back right corner. *Arctic Circle 37564*. Not sure what to make of the letter, I put it off to the side.

"Looks like junk mail or some elaborate prank," I said.

"What about this letter?" Zed asked as he handed it to me.

This one looked expensive and official. It was a bright white envelope with a typewritten return address in the corner. The envelope itself felt stiff. I surmised that the letter had been freshly printed was for a special occasion. Since it was addressed to 'Residents of-' I realized that this letter was sent out to a multitude of people, not just myself. There was a green wax seal on this envelope as well, but this time with flecks of gold.

"Whoever sent this must have some deep pockets," I said.

Dear Current Residents,

The Evergreen Household would like to welcome you to the first annual Evergreen Christmas Party. With this letter, you will be given a ticket with an express pass to Evergreen Manor. Present your ticket to the conductor of the Glacier Express and you will be escorted to the manor. The party begins at 8:00 pm sharp on Christmas Eve. Let the Christmas season move you, and the feelings of joy inhabit you, for it is Christmas and all will be well. We look forward to welcoming you into our humble abode.

Sincerely,
Mr. Alderheim Evergreen

"Hmm? Surprise, surprise, we managed to get an invitation, Zed."

"From whom and to where?"

"Seems the Evergreens invited us to a get-together."

"That rich family in the mountains? Is this because of our last job?"

"Doubtful, it wasn't an invitation to us specifically. Judging by the letter's presentation, this was mass-produced and distributed to multiple people in the area."

"A Christmas party, huh? Sounds lackluster..." Zed said.

I gazed at the invitation before turning my attention to the other threatening letter. I paused, thinking of the timing of the two letters. *Coincidence?*

"Quite the contrary, Zed," I said, forming a smile. "I believe this invitation is just the distraction I have been looking for."

"I guess Christmas came early for us," Zed said.

With that decided, Zed and I began getting ready for a potentially interesting evening.

Thirty minutes later, Zed and I were just about ready to hit the town. Before we left, I stood before a mirror. I was sporting my trademark fedora and low-cut trim with a fade around the side, along with my black trench coat and a pair of leather gloves.

"Gloves, hat, trench coat, and a good-looking dark-skinned guy to tie the whole outfit together," I said to the mirror.

"Don't forget to fix your tie and be sure to wear a scarf." Zed barked.

"Okay mom, sheesh," I said.

It was still the dead of winter, so I made sure to dress appropriately. Meanwhile, Zed wore a burgundy vest with a black bowtie and khaki shorts, and he walked on all fours in the guise of a pet playing dress up. The outfit went well with his black fur. Despite his clothing being short-sleeved and ridiculous-looking on him in his current state, he carried himself with dignity and trotted along the path. Both the weather and the apparent gazes from the passersby did nothing to perturb him.

"It must be nice to have fur," I said.

Zed smirked, fully aware of his winter advantage. Despite that, even I had to admit the burgundy vest really showed off his fur.

The Glacier Express train station was filled to the brim with people trying to make last-minute travel plans on Christmas Eve. From where we stood, I could see many individuals sharing heartfelt reunions as families reconnected with loved ones on last-minute arrivals. Even I couldn't help but feel somewhat moved at the sight of a family of Wolf Beastmen coming together and sharing a moment. The father had come off the train with a haggard expression and, based on his slightly disheveled appearance with his black fur and tie, it must have been a stressful work week. However, all of his weariness faded away as soon as he saw his pregnant wife, sporting white fur, holding onto two pups at the station. The kids themselves were sporting white and black fur, and one of them was playing around with an action figure while the other threatened to snatch it. It only took a few seconds before a tug-of-war broke out. Fortunately, their bickering immediately came to an end when they saw their father approach. They were ecstatic to see him and ran in his direction. Not missing a beat, the Beastman dropped to his knees and extended his arms, hugging them warmly. Soon after, he ran to his wife and pulled her into an embrace as the children joined.

"Oh, how sweet," Zed said, watching the touching moment.

"Let's just hope that the bun in the oven is really his," I said, turning away from the scene.

"Really, man? Must you do this?" Zed said, annoyed.

"Look at the husband's clothes and his expression. He clearly is in business, but based on how exhausted he looked, it is a low-level position. A job like that comes with a lot of stress and not enough money. If that reunion is an indication of anything, it's that he has to travel far from home for his job, which is guaranteed to put stress on any relationship. His travels could give the wife time to be a little promiscuous," I said, trying to maneuver around the horde of people at the station.

"Look, I know the term 'holiday spirit' means nothing to you, but must you rain on everybody's parade?" Zed chided.

"It's an occupational hazard. I see things for what they are."

"Do you really believe that?" Zed asked me.

I turned my head to look back at the couple. This time I saw them walking away from the station hand in hand, staring happily into each other's eyes as they each carried a child. I stared at the scene for a few seconds.

"It's a possibility, hence why I said 'Let's just hope.' Besides, the newborn should have gray fur regardless," I said.

"Wait, what makes you so sure?"

"What do you get when you mix black and white?" I said with a slight smirk.

Zed stared back at me incredulously. "You really know nothing of genetics, do you?" Zed said.

Unfortunately, the happy reunion did nothing to lighten my mood as we traversed the busy train station. The number of times I had to say "excuse me" or "watch it" was ridiculous. Since I already had a ticket, I was able to bypass most of the long lines to see the booking clerk, which was a stroke of good fortune. I headed towards the floating television that showed all of the trains scheduled to depart for Evergreen Manor. As I searched for the train's arrival, smoke from the tracks quickly enveloped the station. Sounds of coughing, snarls, growls, and yells could be heard from the people enveloped by the sudden haze. Zed and I were in the midst of it and tried to cover our mouths. I pulled up the collar of my trench coat to block out the strange smoke. Although, I quickly realized it wasn't smoke that was invading the train station.

"Steam," I said.

Relieved, Zed and I calmly moved further toward the train tracks. The closer we came, the more the steam evaporated around us until we were eventually greeted by the locomotive. The train was jet black and appeared to stretch for miles beyond the station. The heat emanating from the train made it seem almost alive and like it was waiting patiently for a chance to run wild on the track. A few seconds passed until the door to the train flung open and a bespectacled man with a burly mustache appeared. "All aboard!" he yelled. It didn't take long for us to realize that he was the conductor of the train.

"Are you fellas headed to Evergreen Manor?" he asked us with a jovial grin.

"We are." I nodded.

"Well, right this way. Don't be shy and don't worry about your dog, pets ride free of charge," the conductor said with a wink.

The conductor ushered Zed, who wasn't pleased with being considered a pet, and I aboard.

"Sit anywhere you like, fellas," the conductor said.

I tipped my hat to the man and walked down the aisle. While looking for a seat, I noticed that many supposedly upstanding members of society were already aboard. The smell of expensive perfume and constant chattering gossip about supposed affairs, business schemes, and the hottest trends gave them away as upper class. They reeked so potently of frivolity that I felt like gagging. Escaping the peanut gallery, Zed and I finally found unoccupied seats with fewer people around so we'd be able to speak freely away from greedy ears.

A few moments later, the train whistle roared as if it was a wild beast. I stared out the window as the train began to move. Slowly at first, but once we entered the tunnel, the pace rapidly increased. The space warped around us as we shot out of the tunnel like a cannonball.

"Mana-tech has advanced pretty far," I said.

The light that abruptly shone into the window was almost

blinding. Despite the warping speed, the night sky was still visible. The snow was reflected and brightened by the moonlight. I rubbed my eyes and continued to stare out of the window, mindlessly observing the city as the train sped off. Even though Christmas was right around the corner, the townspeople refused to slow down. It seemed like they were working harder ahead of the impending holiday. I couldn't help but feel a tad bit melancholy as we left the city limits and were faced with snowy mountains. I stared out the window, still contemplating how the world has changed so much in the last century. *Was it always like this?*

Hundreds of years ago, humanity was in an all-out war. Nobody knows for sure how it happened or why, but many historians theorized it was due to a nuclear catastrophe. Personally, I'd put my money on a couple of big-wig politicians who were having a ridiculous dispute behind the scenes and the masses were caught in the crossfire. Still, the catalyst for either explanation is unknown. Either way, humanity was on the brink of extinction until monsters, or what we now call *Legends,* resurfaced. Imagine all the stories you heard as a kid—from vampires to werewolves, dragons, and elves—were as real as you and me. Apparently, these Legends have coexisted with humans since ancient times. However, as humans progressed with their rapid technological advancements, the Legends became less prominent. The age of humanity so overshadowed them that they went into hiding. Some went underground, some returned to their home dimension, while others hid in plain sight. Humans had forgotten the Legends almost entirely, remembering them only as fairy tales. Until the war happened.

Evidently, some Legends still sought revenge on the humans

for driving them into hiding. During their world-spanning war, the human population dwindled. When the humans were at their weakest, the Legends broke free and began to wreak havoc on the human population. Humanity tried to fight back, but their attempts were futile. The Legends had an overwhelming advantage. Some of the Legends decided to enslave humans, keeping them as sick trophies to be paraded around. Others were like cattle for slaughter. With Legends officially back on the scene, there was a re-release of a particular substance that was fabled in the olden days. The substance only seemed to make some of them stronger and had a poisonous effect on humans. Some people died from the stress it placed on the body, while others became horribly disfigured. It was literal hell on earth for humanity.

Eventually, a miracle occurred. Humans began adapting to the poisonous substance, though nobody was sure how it was possible. Over time, humans not only adapted, they became enhanced by it. This substance was eventually called *Mana*, as it bestowed upon humans the gift of magic, that we later called *Graces*. Graces are boiled down to two broad categories: Physical and Magical. Physical types are called *Enhanced*. They consist of those with latent bloodlines that awaken varying physical mutations, traits, or superhuman capabilities. Magical types are called *Mages*. They consist of those who can use mysterious abilities that can defy physics.

Despite the newfound power, humans were not adept at wielding it. Not all were gifted with a Grace though, and these individuals were eventually shunned by society. Rumors swirled that those who had not been gifted had instead found their own methods of survival. Those people were called the *Perditius*. Fortunately, not all of the Legends had a bitter disgust for humans, and some went as far as to give humans shelter from hostile elements. Some Legends, for example the Elves, went out of their way to teach the humans how to use their new abilities. Such generosity was unheard of at the time. Other Legends concocted a plan to use their slaves to their advantage. The slaves were put through tortuous experiments to brainwash them and eventually turn them into mindless killing machines. The cruel Legends, inspired by the Elves, taught their humans more sinister ways of using Mana, and even tried to fashion themselves as gods. Many cults and new religions emerged as a result, and the many factions served as inevitable catalysts for yet another war.

Various factions rose up to fight, claiming their "god" was the true one to be served. In reality, this war was not a holy crusade, but a power conflict to determine dominance over the planet. The Elves and the human-supporting Legends, along with their human companions, had no choice but to fight to save the planet from annihilation. The war was catastrophic and lasted a century. All parties suffered horrific casualties, but that death and destruction did nothing to dampen their fighting spirit.

Mysteriously, it's been said a group of powerful ancients came in when enough was enough. The war ended abruptly with no winner, only mutual devastation. Many agreed that such atrocities should never happen again, so a peace agreement was brokered and the world was rebuilt. Despite the calls for peace, some factions scoffed at the terms of the agreement. Some of those factions are represented by today's council members, including Dracula, of the *Vampires*, Cretan II of the *Theriantropes*, and Merlin of the Mages guild. The Djinn are currently represented by the current *Ifrit*. And the others by their respective heads.

Thankfully, those factions separated themselves from the rest in lieu of continued fighting. Not long ago, things returned to a new form of normal where humans lived harmoniously with the myths and legends from history. The post-war progress birthed a new world, which was given a new name as a hallmark of how far everyone had come to achieve peace. Thus, the world was called *Myelv*.

"Bark!" I snapped back to reality. Zed was trying to get my attention.

Turning from the window, I was greeted by a pale hand in front of my face. My eyes followed the long arm back to a beautiful young woman smiling at me. Her eyes were closed and her black hair was tied in a bun underneath a conductor's hat.

"Tickets please," she said.

As she spoke, her eyes opened and I was greeted by multiple black reflective pupils in each eye socket. I felt like I was being watched by several people. Below her eyes, the woman had two sets of fangs in her mouth. When I revealed my ticket, she inspected it for a moment. Then her other spider like arms came from behind her. They each extended to other passengers grabbing their tickets. The hairy arms had punched a hole in the tickets and returned it to me and the others in one smooth motion. Before she moved on, the young woman winked at me. The action was unsettling but I tipped my hat to be polite nonetheless. As she moved further down the aisle, she used her extra arms with frightening efficiency to inspect several tickets at once. Zed waited until the Jorogumo was far enough away to ask, "What had you so zoned out?"

"I was just thinking about the past. No biggie," I said

nonchalantly.

"Right. Well, aside from that, why are we going to Evergreen Manor? Last time I checked you hate Christmas parties almost as much as you hate the holiday itself."

"Maybe I was suddenly infected with the holiday spirit."

"And maybe I am the ghost of Christmas past. Now that we both got our jokes out of the way, how about giving me a real answer?"

"To be honest, I am not too sure myself. But ever since the invitation arrived, I've been wondering why I was invited."

"Didn't you say the letter was sent to a multitude of people?"

"I did at first but, something seems strange with that line of thought."

Zed tilted his head, waiting for me to explain. "Well, even though the letter wasn't addressed to me specifically, I still think someone is calling me out."

"How?"

"Look at the people on this train. We don't exactly scream high society like these folks. Also, at the train station, most of the people were waiting in long lines, but when our train showed up, we were the only ones waiting to get on the train to Evergreen Manor." Zed's ears perked up as I continued.

"That means out of the entire town, only *I* got an invitation to this party. It makes me wonder."

Zed groaned, "So much for a simple night out."

Chapter II

The train came to a full stop when eight o'clock finally rolled around. Zed and I, along with the rest of the passengers, made our way out of the train and was immediately enveloped by steam. With the limited visibility, I wasn't able to take note of my surroundings, but I could see other passengers walking away from the train. Some of them appeared to be familiar with the location, so Zed and I decided to follow the crowd. The further we walked from the locomotive, the more the steam dissipated. After a few more steps, we were standing outside of a huge gate. I couldn't help but whistle in amazement.

"What an enormous gate," I remarked.

Behind me I heard, "Ahem." Looking around, I noticed a man in the booth. Leaving his post, I was greeted by a seven-foot Cyclops wearing a black uniform with a gold shield emblem on the left of his chest. His shaved head and the clipboard in his hands gave him the appearance of the head of security. He eyed me from head to toe with suspicion.

"Is this your first time here?" the guard said gruffly.

"Guilty as charged," I said.

"State your business."

"Well, Mr. Evergreen is hosting a party and I was invited."

"Your ticket please," the guard said, unfazed.

I showed him what had arrived in the mail. He inspected it while checking for confirmation on the clipboard. He soon returned the ticket to me and then turned his attention to Zed.

"Is that furball with you?" he asked, pointing.

Zed growled at the man, causing the one-eyed guard to retract his finger.

"Yes, he is with me. And you would do well not to refer to him as a 'furball,'" I said.

"Well, whatever he is, there are no pets allowed. Leave your mutt out here."

Zed looked about ready to pounce on the one-eyed guard.

"Unfortunately, I can't do that. See, this is my service dog. He helps me with my day-to-day activities," I lied, hugging Zed.

"If I was ever separated from him, I just don't know what I'd do," I explained.

The Cyclops rolled his eye in annoyance.

"Fine, whatever," he said as he pressed the button on the booth, which opened the gate. Zed gave one final growl to the guard before walking through.

Evergreen Manor was huge. The front yard had a wide-open space, and you could clearly see the courtyard and its oddly shaped shrubbery. I'd like to think they were crude depictions of Christmas ornaments. One thing was for sure, they definitely fit the definition of "abstract." Upper-class citizens had more money than they knew what to do with. Before entering the mansion, I had to bring attention to my canine companion.

"Do you mind making yourself look more presentable, please? I would rather not give one of those dignitaries a heart attack at the sight of you."

"Okay, okay," Zed said.

Waving his paw dismissively, my furry four-legged friend stood up on two legs as his fur retracted into his body and his snout shrunk into a human nose. Zed, now having the appearance of a man, scratched his head and tried to adjust his jacket.

"Is this dignified enough for you?" Zed said.

"I'm not so sure about 'dignified,' but at least now we can properly begin the night's festivities."

As we made our way into the mansion, we were greeted by a butler who asked for our jackets. We complied, and Zed snagged us two bottles of water from one of the passing servers. My partner wasted no time downing his drink while I busied myself with observing the other guests.

"Are you sure those two letters are connected?" Zed asked.

"I'm not one hundred percent sure, but based on the timing of those two letters, I'd be willing to bet on it. We just need to find the connection," I explained.

"Should we keep an eye out for anything peculiar, or will the universe just hand it to us on a silver platter?" Zed asked.

"Ha-ha, very funny. I'd rather stick to facts than dumb luck. No, I need you to look out for suspicious people and anyone using the same scentless ink as in the letter," I said.

"Any ideas what our mystery writer wants?" Zed inquired.

"I have a few ideas, but I can't say for certain."

"Okay, but I have one question."

I arched an eyebrow.

"You gonna finish your drink?"

After downing his second drink, Zed offered me a makeshift salute and then we parted ways. After his departure, I returned my attention to the ballroom. It was massive and nearly packed to the brim with wealthy dignitaries with too much free time. The ceiling of the ballroom had a Gothic style to it, with a mural of demons chasing angels. While I appreciated the break from Christmas decor, I was struck by how grim the art looked by comparison. Unfortunately, my appreciation was cut short due to the amount of chatter and nonsense in my surroundings. Unsurprisingly, the guest list was comprised mostly of nobles, dignitaries, and a few rich entrepreneurs. Walking through the crowd, I found that they were all dressed for the season. Some had little ornaments on their ties, while others wore reindeer earrings. I slowly observed the wide-ranging guests, including Half-Orcs, Beastmen, Human elites, Djinn, Elves, and a couple of Dwarves. They all wore highly tailored suits or over-the-top dresses. *Quite a foul assortment of objects*, I thought. I noticed the hall was decorated much the same way, but more vibrantly. There were lights hung up in complex designs and ornaments hanging from the ceiling. I was starting to lose interest in the party's atmosphere.

A man in a green pinstripe suit with a white comb-over was slowly making his rounds from guest to guest. He stood out from the rest and made sure to greet and engage himself with everyone. I presumed that he was our host. I intended to greet him, but I was suddenly stopped by a group of three individuals. They barred my path, each wearing tacky suits. One was large and seemed to be struggling to fit into his suit, which was too tight for his figure. He had a big nose and two large tusks protruded from his mouth. A Warthog Beastman. By the Beastman's side were two short men wearing sunglasses. One looked at me furiously while the other appeared to be scanning the room. The Dwarves appeared to be the Warthog's bodyguards. While they were short, they both looked very sturdy and well-built.

"Who might you be, sir, and how did you get in here?" the Beastman asked.

"I was invited," I said, flashing my invitation.

"The Evergreens should consider who they add to their guest list."

The Beastman told me his name and then took it upon himself to tell his life story. The only thing I was able to register was how inexplicably foul his breath was. With my eyes watering, I said,

"Might I offer you a mint before you go bragging to people?"

"You insolent little-! Do you know who I am!?" the man exclaimed.

"You're a Warthog with no sense of personal hygiene and appear to be going through some difficult financial times but you're still desperately trying to keep up appearances?" I said.

"I am of the lineage of the three hogs who triumphed over the impetuous wolf!" he grumbled.

Definitely a Warthog, I thought and slowly began to clap.

"Bravo, you come from a family that spent the majority of their life running and hiding."

"Why you!" the Warthog screamed.

"Seems someone can't control his temper," I said.

At that moment, the two bodyguards ran to their master's aid. Confronting me, the two Dwarves stacked on top of each other to reach me at eye level.

"You better show some respect to the boss or else," the Dwarf said, shaking his fist.

I tried to hide my amusement at how ridiculous they looked.

"Or else what? Are you going to kick my shins?" I said,

trying to stifle a laugh.

"Am I a joke to you?"

"Only a little bit," I said, making a pinching motion with my hand.

"LITTLE!? That's it, get him!"

Not liking my choice of words, the Dwarves charged at me. I casually moved to the side, sticking my foot out at the last second. The two came tumbling down like a sack of potatoes. At that point, people stared at us.

This is really starting to get embarrassing, I thought.

"Look, sorry about the comment. Why don't we just go about our business in peace?" I said, extending my hand to the Dwarves. My apology fell on deaf ears as I turned toward the Beastman. The Warthog was seething. "I take it you don't plan on letting me off?" I asked.

Ignoring my words, the Beastman got on all fours and prepared to charge at me. Both bodyguards grabbed me by the leg, keeping me in place. I placed a hand in my inner coat pocket, ready to retaliate. I relaxed as I beckoned the Beastman to charge.

Then, like clockwork, the man in the green pinstriped suit placed a hand on my attacker, stopping him. Looking closely, I saw he had cuffs that resembled Christmas trees at his wrists and a tie in the shape of a Christmas tree. His calm and professional demeanor was only surpassed by his sharp emerald eyes.

Quite sharp, I thought.

It didn't take me long to deduce the man was our amicable host, Mr. Evergreen.

"Excuse me, gentlemen, for interrupting, but I am afraid it won't do to fight in here," the man said.

"He started it!" the Warthog lied.

"And I was just about to end it," I said.

"Now, now gentlemen. There is no need for violence. Besides, I have some business with this man," Evergreen said.

"You have business with this guy?" The Warthog was incredulous.

I raised an eyebrow, also surprised by Mr. Evergreen's words.

"Yes, I do. I heard you've recently fallen on some hard times. I would strongly suggest you mind your own business, lest our friends make your circumstances *Grim*," Mr. Evergreen said. The Beastman understood the veiled threat, and beads of sweat formed on his forehead.

"Apologies, we'll be taking our leave," the Warthog said.

With a snap of his fingers, the Dwarves released me. The trio quickly dispersed as if they had seen a ghost. Unsure of what to make of the situation, I went along with Evergreen.

"Allow me to introduce myself, I am-"

"Alderheim Evergreen, the host of this little soirée," I said.

"I see my reputation precedes me," he said.

"Well, it's not every day I meet someone in the business of growing plants."

"Well, that's oversimplifying it. We are the cutting edge in MagiFlora production. We were the first to consistently cultivate grade five mana plants. Which caused our stocks to quadruple," Evergreen said, his face beaming with pride.

"Which would make you a hot commodity in the schools of magic. Wizards, witches, and summoners could make high-grade potions," I said.

"Not only that, but we recently received a couple of mana defense contracts. The world is constantly changing my friend, and we are the future."

"Color me curious, but how exactly were you able to cultivate grade 5 magiflora?" I asked.

Evergreen narrowed his eyes and gave off a sneer. "You can't expect me to give away trade secrets now, do you? But I'll let you in on a hint." Evergreen's hands gave off a faint glow as he gave me a thumbs-up. "It all starts with a green thumb," Evergreen said as the glow from his hand faded. "Your turn," he continued. "How were you able to spot me among the crowd?"

"Your fashion sense gives you away. Not to mention that I saw you greeting multiple guests and how you commanded attention in order to stop a potentially violent discourse. Who else but the host of the party would do that?" I explained.

"Well, of course, but you must understand it simply wouldn't do for a ruckus to break out in the middle of my party. Especially with someone of your caliber," he said.

"You don't need to flatter me. You said you had business with me?" I asked.

"My business with you can wait until after my announcement. I have another guest to attend to. In the meantime, I do hope you'll enjoy the festivities, Mr.-"

"Ah, I'll be sure to enjoy myself then." I waved a hand and Mr. Evergreen turned to leave.

I hadn't learned much from our brief exchange except that Evergreen was familiar with me and had an interest in some kind of business proposal.

"But before I leave," Alderheim grabbed my shoulder, "I'd like to introduce you to my daughter."

An enchanting young lady emerged. Her hair was stark white with aqua undertones and her face was almost cherubic.

She was wearing a long-sleeved white ball gown with a snowflake design. The dress, which certainly complimented her figure, had a slit that revealed a small portion of her legs. Accompanied by a black corset with a prismatic blue pendant. I could tell by her icy blue-eyed stare that she wasn't amused by the introduction and merely responding to her father's beck and call. Alderheim continued, "This is my daughter, Nikola. Nikola, please be a dear and show our esteemed guest around."

"Hmph," she muttered.

Nikola barely looked me in the eyes as she was introduced. More than anything else, she seemed very annoyed by the whole situation. Alderheim then grabbed his daughter by the arm and whispered in her ear. I was only able to hear a few words.

"Be on your best behavior or else," Alderheim whispered and Nikola's attitude shifted from annoyance to concern.

"Okay, you two have fun," Alderheim said before leaving us.

An awkward silence passed between us, as I wasn't sure how to engage the woman. It was clear she didn't want to be near me. Sensing my unease, Nikola attempted to change the mood by formally introducing herself.

"Well, as my father said, I'm Nikola Evergreen. That's Nikola with a 'k', not a 'c.' And you said your name was?"

"I didn't, but it is very nice to meet you. What sort of name is Nikola?" I inquired.

"My mother gave me the name. Apparently, I was named after someone special,"

"Who, Nikola Tesla?" I joked.

"No, but I have heard that joke a lot..." she said.

"Where is your mother?" I asked.

The conversation went cold and Nikola's face turned sour.

She cast her eyes down at the ground.

"She is at rest. My mother died quite some time ago. The doctors believed it was due to stress, This pendant is all I have left of her." she explained.

"I am sorry to hear that."

"I wish she was here sometimes," Nikola said and forced a smile.

The conversation was going south, so I tried to change the subject.

"Why did daddy dearest appoint you to my aid?" I asked.

I thought the harmless change in the topic would help lighten the mood, but it had the opposite effect. The forlorn smile on Nikola's face vanished. Instead, Nikola furrowed her eyebrows as she gave a deep frown.

"That's my father for you. He's always been a bit of a slave driver."

Nikola took a moment to relax her features, then continued, "He's always been strict and overbearing."

"Well, it's natural for a father to be overprotective of his daughter, especially for someone so influential," I explained.

"Hah. I wonder about that," Nikola scoffed.

"What's there to think about?"

"Because I find myself wanting to escape and be free from all of this," Nikola said, gazing at the guests.

"All of what?" I inquired.

"People don't understand what it's like being suffocated with this immense responsibility. Many assume that since I'm from a well-off family, I have nothing to worry about. But being an heiress to the family is nowhere near as glamorous as you might think," she explained, her hands trembling slightly. When I looked closer, I saw faint scars around her left wrist, though the cuff of her dress hid most of it. Realizing I saw something I shouldn't have; I also turned my attention to the guests.

"So, you're a princess locked in a castle, waiting for your prince charming," I said.

She let out a small laugh.

"I suppose that's one way to look at it," she said, amused.

"What way would you look at it?" I asked.

"I'd call it living in a dollhouse," she said.

"Sounds like a lot of window dressing. Although, is it really all bad?"

"What do you mean?"

"You live lavishly. With your dad's money, you could at least buy whatever you want," I added.

"Yes, but at what cost?"

I felt a slight chill behind those words. Before I was able to say anything else, she spoke again. "This is getting boring. How about we talk about something else?"

Taken aback by Nikola's shift, I was reluctant to say anything at all. Every topic I had brought up had made the conversation more problematic. Silence was better than this.

"You're not much of a conversationalist, are you?" she said.

"I've never been a fan of small talk," I said.

"Then why did you decide to come to a party?"

"I was invited, obviously," I said plainly.

"What's your interest in my father?"

"It's only natural that a guest wishes to inquire about their host," I said dismissively.

"Is that really the truth?" she said, staring at me.

"What makes you think otherwise?" I asked.

Nikola paused as she rolled her eyes at me. "You've looked

bored since the moment you entered the ballroom, and you don't seem to know anyone here. I saw you nearly fight with one of our guests. You spoke to my father like you had business with him. I can tell by your questions about him that you must not know him personally, which is strange because my father does seem to know you. Perhaps you've acquired some degree of fame? That could explain why you haven't given me your name yet. So, I ask again, why are you really here?"

Not bad, I thought.   I snatched a bottle of water from a passing server in order to collect my thoughts. I was at a loss for words.

"So, I caught your attention when I walked into the room? That's not weird at all," I teased.

"I was getting bored having to constantly listen to rich guys brag about their 'car sizes.' Naturally, my attention shifted," she sighed before continuing on, "now stop trying to change the topic."

"What do you mean? You're the one saying how much I stood out and caught your eye."

"Don't flatter yourself. Are you going to answer my question or not?"

Faced with her question, I looked overhead and saw a band preparing their instruments. Noticing this, I smiled at Nikola and extended my right hand out to her, and said,

"I'm here because I believe something interesting will happen."

Chapter III

Then the orchestra began to play. The music surrounded us as guests made their way to the dance floor. Nikola, still confused by my declaration, stared at my hand.

"Is this your way of asking me to dance?" she asked.

"Are you saying you don't want to?" I said.

With a coquettish grin, Nikola grabbed my hand. "Why the sudden interest in dancing with me? Have I caught your eye now?" she teased.

"Nonsense, I just felt this conversation needed a change," I explained.

I led Nikola to the dance floor with her hand in mine. Excitedly, she pulled me toward the center of the dance floor. I was taken aback by this sudden move. We became the center of attention. I felt a bit nervous sharing the limelight with the young heiress. I never did care for being in the spotlight.

"Are you getting cold feet?" Nikola teased.

Taking that as a challenge, I held her close and we positioned ourselves. The music started slow and our movements were stiff, as if we had two left feet.

"For all that bravado, you're really not much of a dancer," Nikola said.

"It's a little hard to do when we're both trying to lead," I explained.

"If that is the case then you should take char-"

Immediately, I put my arm around her waist and pulled her in close. A slight blush rose from Nikola's cheeks. Our faces were only inches apart. We waltzed around the room a few times, and I kept my focus on all the other guests around us.

"If I was your date, I'd feel a bit jealous," Nikola said.

"Huh?"

"Here I am dancing with you, yet your attention is obviously elsewhere. This is a romantic dance where you need to pay attention to your partner," Nikola explained.

Then she held out her hand and turned my head to face her cool blue eyes. She gave a disarming smile. There was something about that smile that made me weak in the knees.

"That's better," the young heiress said.

The dance went on for a while and the music picked up speed. It was a good thing too, because I was beginning to feel myself being hypnotized.

"Can you dance to fast songs too or was that just a one-time deal?" Nikola asked.

"Just make sure you can keep up," I said.

Let's see how good you really are, I thought.

As if reading my mind, Nikola glided onto the dance floor and we began to tango in rhythm. She moved sharply, like a blade twirling in my hands. I followed and matched her speed. Like a sword fight, we moved across the floor in perfect synchrony. It was a unique dance, and it felt as if we were the only two in the room. She went on as if the entire ballroom was a stage for her to command, and everyone else was just a spectator admiring her. In the corner of my eye, I noticed that a few people had stopped dancing just to watch us perform. Even though I was leading, I had to be sure to keep up with her performance to not make a fool of myself. But to her, this seemed like any other day. I was so busy making sure our dance went smoothly that I hadn't noticed the song came to an end. Everyone was staring at us in awe. After a moment of silence, the crowd erupted into applause.

"You're a pretty good dancer," Nikola said.

"You're not so bad yourself," I said.

As the applause ended, the sound of a slow clap reverberated behind us.

"Oh dear," I said in trepidation.

"Well, well, well. While I'm hard at work, my own partner is busy fraternizing with the host's daughter. Seriously, what kind of guest are you?" Zed said with a broad grin.

"This isn't what it looks like," I said.

"Really? Then what would you call two people sharing an intimate moment?" Zed asked.

"It was just a dance," I said.

"Seemed to me you were enjoying it a little too much for it to be just a dance," Zed teased.

"It was the best vantage point," I argued.

The banter between Zed and I went on for a moment. We continued our tomfoolery until Nikola interjected.

"Um, excuse me," she said.

"Ah yes, where are my manners? The name is Zed. And you are?" Zed held out his hand.

"Nikola Evergreen." Nikola accepted his hand.

"Enchanté," Zed said as he kissed her hand.

"I see you're quite the charmer," she said.

"Oh, stop it. But I must thank you for bringing my friend

out to the dance floor," Zed said.

"Actually, the idea was all his," Nikola said.

"Oh, really?" Zed turned to me with a wide grin.

I rolled my eyes, finding the conversation between the two quite troublesome.

"Miss Nikola, I must ask, what is that enchanting scent?" Zed asked as he sniffed Nikola from her hand to her shoulder.

Nikola's face was flushed. Instinctively, I grabbed Zed by the collar and pulled him away from her.

"I am terribly sorry for my friend's behavior," I said.

"It's fine, though usually I get mauled by dogs and not men," Nikola said.

If only she knew, I thought.

Before I could chastise Zed further, a chime echoed throughout the room. We turned to see where the sound came from and saw Mr. Evergreen signaling for everyone's attention.

"Looks like Father is getting ready for his grand speech. I'd better go to his side," Nikola sighed.

"I guess being the heiress to the Evergreen Estate isn't all sunshine and rainbows," Zed said.

"You have no idea," Nikola said.

"Just be sure you hurry along. We'll be here when you get back," I said, giving a thumbs up.

Nikola regained her smile as she took her leave. "I won't keep you waiting too long," Nikola waved.

When I was sure Nikola was gone, Zed and I came together for a conference.

"What the hell was that stunt, Zed?" I asked.

"I was keeping my nose out, just like you said."

"Explain?"

"She smelled weird. That's the reason I sniffed her like that."

"Weird in what way?"

"I kept smelling traces of fear on the girl."

"What was she afraid of?" I asked.

"I don't know. I thought she was afraid of you for a second, but that fear wasn't present while you were dancing. But that's not the strangest part."

"What's the strangest part then?"

"For some reason, I can't smell anything of the girl other than a faint trace of fear and some expensive perfume. I can't smell her own individual scent. It's almost like she is hiding it. Honestly, if I was just going by my nose, I probably would've never noticed her," Zed explained.

Lost in thought, I tried to understand what Zed said. Before I could piece any of this information together, a crowd gathered in the center of the ballroom, awaiting Mr. Evergreen's speech. All eyes were on our host, with Nikola at her father's side.

"Hello everyone," he said. "I would like to thank you all for coming here today to visit my family and help us celebrate this holiday season. Today is a day where we all put our differences aside, regardless of if you are of the human variety or the more inhuman kind. This world we live in is ever-changing, but one thing that stays the same is Christmas. It is the one time of year that we can end discrimination and stop the bloodshed and feuds that plague us throughout the year. So, let it be known that today, the leaders in each faction were able to come together and show that they are much more than the monsters that society portrays them to be. Now, let us count down to the day that will always be remembered in our hearts." After finishing his speech, Mr. Evergreen pressed a button on a remote.

Suddenly, the floor below us opened and a giant clock rose up from out of it.

"This guy really loves to show off his wealth," I remarked to Zed.

The time on the clock was eleven fifty-nine PM. A particularly short, well-dressed man with slicked-back gray hair and pointy ears approached Mr. Evergreen and whispered something into his ear. Mr. Evergreen raised an eyebrow and quickly walked away from his guests' eyes. He gave a few solid handshakes and soft waves to the people. As Evergreen walked further away from his guests, he appeared to be on high alert to make sure he wasn't being followed. Meanwhile, the guests became excited as the clock began its countdown. Sixty seconds appeared on the clock.

"Fifty-eight!" the people shouted.

Escaping the crowd, I was curious about where Evergreen had to go in such a hurry.

"You're planning to go follow him?" Zed asked.

"He did say he had business with me. Besides, it wouldn't hurt to do a little snooping. Apologize to Nikola for me," I said.

"No problemo," Zed said.

"Forty-two!" the crowd shouted.

Zed turned his attention to the crowd as I attempted to follow Mr. Evergreen. However, before I took a step, I was greeted by the young heiress.

"Nikola?" I said.

"Where are you going?" she asked.

Flustered, I tried to give a convincing excuse. However, before I could mutter anything, Nikola grabbed me by the arm and pulled me closer to the clock.

"Thirty-eight!" the crowd continued.

"The countdown has begun. We should find a nice spot for the show," Nikola said, excited.

I tried to think of a way to excuse myself from the situation. Unfortunately, no immediate solution came to mind. As I was pulled towards the crowd of people with Nikola at my side, I reunited with Zed. He raised his eyebrow at the sight of Nikola and I together.

On his face was a look that said, *Back so soon?*

I pointed to Nikola to explain, *She got in the way.*

Worried his trail might grow cold, I signaled Zed to follow Mr. Evergreen. Zed nodded his head and immediately gave chase. It was difficult for me to think while Nikola and the rest of the crowd cheered.

"Twenty-eight!"

A few seconds later, Zed returned to my side looking dejected.

"I lost him," Zed whispered.

"What do you mean?" I whispered.

"Twenty-five!" the crowd continued to shout.

"I mean the guy went *poof* and turned into a ghost," Zed explained.

"You can't track him by smell?"

"I never got his scent and there are too many people around. I'd be flying blind."

"Wait a minute, Evergreen patted me on the shoulder earlier. Would that work?" I asked.

"Scents don't work like that. Even if they did, your scent would've overtaken his by now."

"Oh Zed, you made it just in time with only a few more seconds left till the show!" Nikola cheered.

Time was running out and Zed and I lost track of Mr.

Evergreen. I was lost in thought among the cheers. Something about the whole situation didn't sit right with me. I had a sneaking suspicion that something terrible would happen at midnight.

Why would the host leave his party so soon? What did Evergreen want to discuss with me?

The questions swarmed in my mind.

"Twenty!" the crowd shouted.

"So, what kind of show are we in for?" Zed asked Nikola.

"Nineteen!"

"I don't know, honestly, but I'm sure it will be one to remember," Nikola answered.

"Eighteen!"

"I don't doubt that for a second," I said.

"Seventeen!"

The crowd grew more excited and began to huddle together more closely. Zed and I were getting pushed into each other.

"Well, this is uncomfortable," Zed said.

"Sixteen!"

"Agreed," I said.

"Fifteen!"

Annoyed, Zed began to look for a way out of the crowd and their shouting. He took my hand and tried to lead us out. I reached out for Nikola's hand but found nothing. When I turned around, I found only a group of random strangers next to me.

"Zed, is Nikola near you?"

"I thought she was near you."

At that moment he and I realized something very important.

"Nikola disappeared!" Zed and I said in unison.

"Where the heck did she go?" I asked.

"Fourteen!"

"How should I know? I thought you were watching her," Zed said.

"Thirteen!"

"She probably got lost in the crowd. Let's just split up and find her."

"Ten!"

"Got it."

Zed and I had separated to try and find Nikola in the midst of the chaos. The crowd kept on shouting.

"Five, four, three, two, one!"

I took one more glance at the clock. Midnight.

"MERRY CHRISTMAS!" the crowd erupted.

All around me, people began hugging each other. Some shared drinks of brandy and eggnog. Zed and I continued to search for Nikola, but to no avail. As the crowd dispersed, Zed and I met up with each other, both shaking our heads. Then we heard a loud shriek. It was somewhere between a high-pitched power saw and nails on a chalkboard, and it reverberated throughout the manor. Not wanting to waste any time, Zed and I dashed in the direction of the scream.

"Let's go," I signaled Zed.

Zed got on all fours, transformed into his hound form, and I saddled up. We rushed into action.

Act II

Chapter IV

We heard sobbing coming from the other side of an open door. Immediately, Zed and I entered to find Nikola crying. She was unharmed, but tears were pouring from her eyes as she hugged herself in the corner of the room.

"H-h-how did this happen?" Nikola stuttered.

"What happened?" I asked.

"Over here," Zed called out.

I turned around to find Mr. Alderheim Evergreen's body on the floor. It was devoid of all life. I scanned the area for important clues or signs of a struggle. As I looked around the room, a group of people nearly swarmed in to see the fresh corpse. Zed snarled, driving them back, so don't disturb the crime scene. Nikola was still in complete shock, so I placed my jacket around her shoulders to calm her down.

Suddenly, a tall man with a scraggly beard approached me from out of the crowd.

"Hello, I am Joe Turner," the man said. "I am a reporter for the *Everyday Monster Weekly*."

"EMW? What's a reporter doing here so soon?" I asked.

"Well aside from the free drinks, my associate and I got a hot tip Evergreen would be making a grand reveal. I came down here to see if I could get an exclusive."

EMW was just one of the many news sources in the area. They weren't as big as some of the major news outlets, but I had followed a few of their stories in the past. Their news stories ranged from trend pieces and entertainment to corruption.

"What announcement?" I asked.

"Didn't you hear? Alderheim threw this huge Christmas celebration to reveal some new developments to the Evergreen estate," Turner explained.

"So, what do you want with me? Are you looking for a statement?"

Turner pointed to the crowd of people he came with.

"Turns out the group of people over there voted for me to take the lead, seeing as our previous host just kicked the bucket," Turner explained.

I took a good look at Joe Turner. Despite the scraggly beard and somewhat disheveled appearance, he constantly stood up straight and maintained good posture with his feet close together. His fiery red eyes that told me he was no stranger to danger. I reached to shake the man's hand and I was impressed by his firm grip. On the side of his right arm he had a picture of a shield and a bird.

Is he a veteran? I wasn't sure what to make of the reporter, but one mystery at a time.

"Good, call the police and make sure no one gets in and contaminates the crime scene," I ordered.

Turner nodded but before he left he asked, "The people have been asking who you are. What am I supposed to tell them?"

"The name is Kai, Detective Kai."

After the pleasantries, Turner directed the guests to take their leave to allow me to work the scene. Nikola followed the group. Zed escorted her, as she was still shaken up. As I was about to inspect the body, Joe Turner rushed back into the room.

"I called the police. Unfortunately, there's a massive blizzard outside," Turner said.

"What?" I exclaimed.

I turned my attention to a window and saw that a fierce blizzard was howling outside. The storm had really picked up too and had knocked down some trees. All I could see outside was snow and turbulent winds.

"Because of the weather, the authorities won't be able to come until the morning," I surmised.

"Did I mention the worst part of it yet?" Joe asked.

Joe pointed further in the distance. It was hard to make out, but there was a pack of wolves out there. They looked hungry and their glowing yellow eyes were staring daggers at Evergreen Manor. A chorus of howls reverberated outside, shaking the glass window.

"As you can see, Detective, not only are we barred from outside support-"

"We are also trapped here like rats," I said.

"I already told everyone to refrain from going outside. We even took steps to bar the door so nothing can get in or out," Turner explained.

"Did you notice anyone trying to make their way to the main exit?" I asked.

"Not really. People are mostly hoping for the police to arrive."

"When you told the people about the storm, did anyone look upset or annoyed by the blizzard?"

"Not exactly. They mostly seemed scared."

"Now things are looking like a proper murder mystery," I said.

Joe looked at me incredulously while I rubbed my hands together with a smile. I was intrigued with how the night was turning out.

"Keep watch over the guests and bring Zed back in. He is the one currently on all fours," I said.

Without further distractions, I put on a pair of white gloves and kneeled down to examine the corpse of Mr. Evergreen. There weren't any external wounds, though there seemed to be a splatter of blood and a black substance around his lips. His Adam's apple was a bit strange too. It looked as if there was a protruding lump or sore there, causing it to bulge out.

"How strange," I said.

I parted the corpse's lips and plunged my hand down the man's esophagus. At the worst possible time, Joe had returned with Zed.

"Here is your faithful companion, Detec-!?"

Turner said before the sight of my whole hand inside a dead man's mouth stopped the words on his tongue. Zed raised an eyebrow.

"Look, I can explain," I said tentatively.

"Sadly, I've been with you long enough to be used to this," Zed said.

"Then do you mind explaining it to someone who hasn't?" Joe asked.

"I was examining the body and I realized that something was stuck in the victim's throat. I'm trying to see what it is," I explained and resumed tugging on whatever had been deeply lodged in his throat. Joe looked disgusted, but after a few tugs and a wet popping noise, I managed to remove the obstruction.

"What the hell?" I said.

All three of us stared in wide-eyed confusion at the Christmas stocking in my hands. It was still wet with blood and saliva from the victim's mouth.

"Is this a joke?" Zed asked.

Turning the stocking over, I looked inside and found a lump of coal. The three of us exchanged a glance, dumbfounded as to how a lump of coal, inside a stocking, had made it inside the victim's throat.

"Any ideas, Detective?" Joe asked.

The question had me stumped. I took a moment to think as query after query bombarded my mind.

"Well, given the lack of external wounds and no signs of a struggle, we have no choice but to assume Mr. Evergreen choked to death on a stocking filled with coal."

As ridiculous as that sounded we had no choice but to accept that as fact.

"How the hell did this happen?" Zed asked.

"Still working on that," I answered.

"Wow, talk about a real stocking stuffer," Joe joked.

Zed and I gave Joe a chilling response. Under normal circumstances, I would have rebuked such a joke. However, my mind was too busy trying to uncover the truth of this case. After a moment of thought, I searched in the stocking and discovered something else. Inside, there was a folded piece of paper along with the coal. The letter had a mistletoe design inscribed on the paper. I recognized it immediately. When I unfolded the letter, I saw words written in familiar handwriting.

> ***Oh, dear child, did I not forewarn thee?***
> ***Naughty boys are only worth their lump sum in coal.***

I flipped the letter around for more writing, but saw nothing. Then I beckoned Zed over.

"Sniff this," I asked him.

Zed closed his eyes and took a whiff of the paper. After a few moments, he scrunched up his face in disgust. I couldn't imagine what kind of scents were passing through his nose.

"What's the matter? Did you find something?" I asked.

"That's just it. Besides the usual smell of blood and bile mixed with coal, I got nothing," Zed said.

"What do you mean, nothing?" Joe asked.

"I meant I couldn't get an identifying scent from the letter."

"Wait, so the letter is-"

"Scentless, that's exactly what he means," I interjected.

After a moment, I pulled out the letter I had received earlier that day from my pocket and compared it to what I'd just found. The two letters had many similarities, from the handwriting, to the ink, to the design of the paper. However, there was one difference.

"It seems like whoever wrote the first letter also wrote the second. It's the same format for the most part," I explained.

"That would explain how I wasn't able to smell anything. They must be using the same scentless ink as before," Zed affirmed.

"In other words, whoever wrote this is our murderer?" Joe inquired.

"That seems to be a good first theory, but still too soon to say for certain," I said.

Putting away the letters, I inspected the rest of the room. Following my lead, Zed sniffed the body first and then explored all around the room. It was a typical private office. There was a couch for visitors and a desk with a computer. Of course, no office in a respectable manner would be complete without its very own fireplace.

Two things that stood out in the room. The first was the fireplace with logs that had been recently burnt to a crisp. When I stuck my hand inside I could feel some residual warmth within.

"The fire was recently extinguished," I mumbled.

The other area of interest was on the victim's desk. On top was a plate with some crumbs and a glass with a drop of white liquid. I used my handkerchief to inspect the glass. I dipped part of my handkerchief inside the glass to taste a small sample.

"Milk?" I said, puzzled.

Then I turned to the plate with crumbs on it. I sat back in the desk chair, lost in thought, and stroked my chin. I was trying to piece everything I found together until—

"KAI!" Zed shouted, nearly sending me off the chair.

"What?" I shot back, annoyed.

"You were making scary faces while you were thinking again."

Apparently, I tend to make an intimidating face when I'm lost in thought.

"So, you figure out who did it yet?" Joe asked.

I paused for a moment drumming my fingers on the desk.

"First things first, we need to do something about Evergreen's corpse."

"Can't we just move it?" Joe asked.

"Not exactly, we can't risk damaging the crime scene before the police arrive." Zed answered.

"For now, let's try covering the body with a sheet or something. We may have to do something about the smell later, but this is the best we can do. In the meantime," I turned towards Joe, "can you go fetch Nikola for me?"

Joe Turner arched an eyebrow at my request but nodded his head.

I was mulling over the case while Zed looked around the room when Joe Turner arrived with the lady, who was still terribly shaken up. Though I didn't want to, I thought it was important to question the tearful heiress.

"Miss, I have a few questions for you," I tried to be as gentle as possible when speaking to her. She nodded, ready to answer my inquiries.

"How did you find your father in such a state?" I asked.

Nikola shook a little bit with hesitation. Clearly, she appeared to be traumatized by the event. After a few moments, she took a deep breath and spoke.

"After my father left the ballroom, I decided to look for him. I figured he was in his study, as this is where he spends most of his free time. When I went to check the door, it was locked. So…" Nikola paused and gripped her arms in an attempt to soothe herself. I urged her to continue.

"Please, Nikola, the faster you tell us what happened the sooner we'll apprehend the culprit."

She collected herself for the time being and then continued her retelling.

"The…the room was locked, I knocked on the door and called out to my father several times but there was no response. So I got the spare key from his secret hiding place. It's underneath the potted evergreen tree on the right of the door."

"And what did you see?" I asked.

"After I opened the door, I saw…I saw…" Nikola was struggling to keep herself together. Her emotions seemed to have a firm grip on her throat. "I saw my father lying there.

He wasn't moving."

"You found your father's body alone? Was there anyone else there with him or with you?" I asked.

"I only saw his body on the ground," she said, hugging herself and shuddering at the memory.

"You didn't even see a silhouette or anything?" Zed asked.

"No, whoever did this was long gone by the time I entered." Nikola paused and wiped her eyes.

"Why would someone do this?"

Nikola looked as if she was going to give into her emotions at any moment, and it was clear this conversation was taking its toll on her. I needed to wrap up the interrogation quickly.

"One more question," I said.

"Yes?"

"Did your father have a sweet tooth?" I asked.

Nikola gave a look of surprise as she stammered to answer the question.

"N-no, not really, but what does that have to do with-"

I smiled at the Heiress as I placed a hand on her shoulder and led her to the door.

"Thank you for your time. If you need anything, Joe Turner has been appointed as a temporary leader. He'll be happy to attend to you."

"Hey, wait a minute," Joe said.

"Oh yes, Joe, can you gather all the maids and servants? I'd like to ask them a couple of questions as well. I'm sure Miss Nikola can help you find them." I closed the door abruptly before Joe could voice a complaint.

"Come along, Zed. We have work to do."

"I take it you've come up with a theory?" Zed asked.

"I still need more evidence before I'm ready to commit to

either, no matter how absurd," I said.

"Absurd?" Zed asked.

Chapter V

Before I could explain, the two heavily contrasting maids arrived. The first one was a Beastman of the goat variety. She had snow-white fur which complimented her Victorian maid's uniform and gave her an angelic appearance. Although her goat eyes were a little out of place as were her small and protruding horns. The second maid was much shorter than the Beastman and was dressed in a Lolita maid's uniform. When she moved closer, I noticed this maid wasn't organic at all but appeared to be a living marionette. The doll had blondish-white hair and a round face. On her lips was a bright red lipstick. The doll's face was devoid of emotion and her hollow blue eyes stared at me dully. I couldn't tell if the doll was indifferent or giving a piercing glare towards me. Though I found her gaze a little unsettling, I was intrigued by the fresh faces in front of me.

"Hello. My name is Elizabeth Kapro and this is Mary," the Beastman introduced herself and the doll. Not wanting to be rude, I introduced myself.

"Ah yes, my name is Kai, I'm-"

"We know all about you, sugar," Elizabeth interrupted.

"Excuse me?" I said.

I wondered how these maids, who I had never met, knew

me. Mary, who remained silent, twirled around and danced. It took me a second to realize what was happening, and when I did, I sank back into the chair, feeling my cheeks turn red.

"Yeah that's it, Mary. We remember you were the one dancing with Lady Nikola," Elizabeth cheered.

"You really put on a show on the dance floor, huh?" Zed teased.

I ignored Zed's provocation as Elizabeth continued, "I have to say, it has been a long while since Lady Nikola smiled like that."

Elizabeth seemed truly relieved at the thought. However, it was still bittersweet as that smile came at the cost of something horrific.

"Of course, now all that happiness is gone because of what's happened to her father," Elizabeth said, seemingly on the verge of tears herself.

Mary's eyes darted around the room for a moment before returning in my direction. I wasn't sure if that was her way of conveying sorrow or if it was something else.

"Ahem!" I cleared my throat to get back on topic.

"Sorry, sugar. I just got to thinking about what Lady Nikola is going through. It makes me wish I could give her a big hug," Elizabeth said.

"Yes, well, if you know all that then you must know why I brought you here."

"Of course. Lady Nikola told us that you are here to investigate the murder and that we should cooperate fully."

"Good. You can start by telling me where you were at the time of the murder," I asked.

"Mary and I were tending to the guests in the ballroom. It wasn't easy for us and the rest of the staff, especially since some were still excited by the performance you and milady gave."

"What about during the countdown?"

"If you thought your dancing got the people so hot and bothered, oh sweet Cretan! People just got more excited when they were huddling together and counting down the last seconds until Christmas. The crowd of people almost crushed me."

"Just like we were," Zed said.

"So you were too stuck in the crowd to see anything," I sighed.

I was becoming annoyed that the maids had nothing more to add, but then Elizabeth spoke.

"I was almost crushed, but if it wasn't for Mary I would have never been able to escape," Elizabeth said happily while petting Mary's head.

Mary showed no visible reaction and continued to stare to the left. I remembered how dense the crowd was when Zed and I were trying to comb through the horde of cheering people.

"How the heck did you manage to escape that dense crowd?" Zed asked.

"More importantly, how did Mary help you to escape the dense crowd?" I added.

How did this doll navigate such an immense crowd while Zed's sense of smell faltered? The thought persisted in my head. The logic just didn't make sense.

Suddenly, Mary got up from the chair and struck a pose. I raised an eyebrow at Mary, not sure what to interpret from the doll's sudden posture. Before I could ask, I saw strings appear to be seeping out of Mary. Elizabeth explained, "Mary has this special thing about her."

I narrowed my eyes at Elizabeth's remark, unsure what to make of it.

"It will be better if we show you," Elizabeth said.

Elizabeth rose from her chair and attempted to strike the same pose as Mary. It was nowhere near as striking and poised as Mary's posture. However, at that moment, the strings seeping out of Mary rushed towards Elizabeth and disappeared behind her. Whatever was lacking in Elizabeth's posture immediately corrected itself and the two began to mirror each other. Then the two maids began to dance in perfect sync. They completely flowed with each other's movements with not a single mistake or lag time between them.

"How are you doing this?" Zed asked.

"Mary can use her strings to latch onto someone and have them mimic her movements. This is how I was able to escape being crushed by the crowd in the ballroom" Elizabeth explained while continuing to dance.

"I see. Mary used her Grace to help you glide through the crowd without getting hurt. I assume the link she can create isn't limited to dancing?" I said.

"More or less, sugar," Elizabeth responded.

Two thoughts persisted while the maids' dance continued: *Where were the strings and how did no one notice them? Normally, a crowd of people would notice someone tethered to a doll.* The two continued to twirl, and I saw no hindrance of the strings impeding either performance. I thought it was strange until I looked down at the floor and understood.

"Seems like you noticed it, sugar," Elizabeth said with a laugh. Their performance came to an end and they both bowed.

"We call her Grace *Shadow Theater*," Elizabeth said.

"Why do you call it that?" Zed asked.

"Look down, Zed," I said.

Once he did, he saw their shadows connected by the strings, which explained how the skill was used covertly.

"Of course it would take a detective to figure that out. Most people never pay attention to what's in their shadows," Elizabeth chuckled.

"We've noticed," Zed grinned.

Mary remained silent and stoic, though she continued to stare in my direction. The strings released themselves from Elizabeth's shadow and returned to Mary. Elizabeth's posture also returned from being elegantly similar to Mary's to something slightly more casual.

"So, with the help of Mary, you avoided being trapped in the crowd during the countdown?" Zed asked.

"Yes, I was trying to get more refreshments for the guests. Unfortunately, they were so excited that Mary and I couldn't return to the crowd. We had to wait patiently for the countdown to come to an end and for the crowd to disperse," Elizabeth explained.

A thought occurred after hearing Elizabeth's testimony. *They were outside the crowd of people.* I then asked Elizabeth if either of them saw anybody else escape from the crowd.

"The only person we saw leaving the crowd was Miss Nikola. Well, maybe besides Mr. Evergreen, who left immediately after his speech and just before the crowd gathered in front of the giant clock," Elizabeth answered.

I asked if they knew the reason both parties left around that time. Unfortunately, neither of the maids had any idea why Mr. Evergreen left when he did. However, Elizabeth noted that Mr. Evergreen seemed to have been in a hurry and was regularly checking his watch. Fortunately, they seemed to be able to speak about Nikola's disappearance.

"We saw Miss Evergreen. I approached her and asked if there was anything we could do for her. She said no and seemed a bit nervous, I wondered if it was because of the passionate dance the two of you shared," Elizabeth paused to make googly eyes at me.

"Miss Nikola told us she needed to check on something. She seemed unsure. Before I could ask anything else, she ran off and told us to make sure we continued to tend to the guests," Elizabeth finished.

I gestured to her, asking if that was all she had to say, but she only nodded.

"Was there anyone in the crowd that looked suspicious?" I asked.

Mary pointed her finger at Zed and I.

Elizabeth explained, "Well, there was a bit of a commotion in the crowd. Apparently, one guest was sniffing around and walking on all fours. The first time it happened was when Mr. Evergreen left, and the second time was after Miss Nikola left."

Zed, who was now in his hound form, couldn't help but smile sheepishly at the maid's comments about him. I pinched the bridge of my nose in annoyance. Otherwise, the maids had nothing else to report about the guests of the party. Pivoting, I asked about the late host. "How was Mr. Evergreen during the day?"

"Well," Elizabeth paused for a moment before recounting the details, "Mr. Evergreen was his usual self during the morning. He had the typical breakfast in the dining room, along with his cup of coffee and the morning paper. Things were normal until the butler gave the mail to Mr. Evergreen. After that, Mr. Evergreen's attitude completely shifted and he retreated to his study."

"I guess you guys have no idea what was in the letters he received?" Zed asked. Elizabeth shook her head.

"Did Mr. Evergreen have a habit of locking himself in his office?" I asked.

"Yes, Mr. Evergreen was an investor and had many business associates come in and out of the place to talk about business. Normally, he locked the door to prevent unwanted intrusions," Elizabeth said.

"You never served Evergreen in his office?" I asked.

"On the occasions that we did it was usually only Mr. Evergreen. Rarely, when the guests were inconsequential to his work, he would leave the door unlocked," Elizabeth said.

"What did you do when the door was locked?" Zed asked.

"We would tell the butler and he would bring Mr. Evergreen his meals when he was ready," Elizabeth answered.

How odd, I thought.

"Why didn't you just use the spare key to enter the room?" I asked.

Both maids exchanged a glance before turning to me. Elizabeth knitted her eyebrows and Mary tilted her head in a very unnatural and doll-like fashion.

"What key are you talking about, sugar? We were never told there was a key," Elizabeth said.

They didn't know? But why? I thought.

"Did anyone visit Mr. Evergreen the day before or during the week?" I asked.

Both maids shook their heads. Nobody had visited the day

before and anyone that had visited during the week was there for a casual visit. We didn't make much headway with that line of inquiry.

"Where was Nikola during the daytime?" I asked.

"Miss Nikola in her room most of the time. She usually elects to eat her meals there. Even though they live under the same roof, Miss Nikola rarely interacts with her father. The moments they interact, the tension between them is almost palpable," Elizabeth said.

I understood Elizabeth's words after I had gotten a slight glance at the dynamic between Nikola and her father during the party. However, since we were on the topic of family interaction, I asked, "What happened to Nikola's mother?"

The two women exchanged looks with each other.

"We heard that she died suddenly but don't know much more than that. Her mother passed away before we were hired. If you want to know about her, the head butler is your best bet," Elizabeth answered.

While Elizabeth was speaking, Mary had her eye turned in Elizabeth's direction. This action was as if she was checking Elizabeth's statement. However, I decided to focus on the murder, not on the eccentricities of a doll.

"One last question," I said.

"Anything, sugar," Elizabeth said.

"How did Mr. Evergreen like his coffee?" I asked.

The look of confusion was plastered on her face. Even Zed raised an eyebrow at my question.

"I believe he liked it black. Why?" Elizabeth answered.

A slight smile washed over my face. "Thank you, ladies, you have been most helpful. Now if you could tell Joe Turner to send the head butler for me, please," I said.

Zed left my side to escort the two maids out of the room. Before Mary got up to leave with Elizabeth, she exchanged a glance at me that turned her eye to the left of the room before turning around in an elegant yet stiff doll-like fashion towards the door. As the maids exited the room and the door closed, Zed turned to me and asked, "So what did we learn?"

"What do you mean?" I said, feigning ignorance.

"Don't act stupid. I know that look. You've figured something out, haven't you?" Zed asked.

"I may have a few ideas, but nothing concrete," I said.

After a few minutes, there was a knock at the door.

"Come in," I announced.

Joe opened the door and walked in with an older gentleman with slicked-back gray hair and pointy ears. He was dressed conservatively, wearing a Victorian tailcoat with nicely tailored pants, formal black shoes, and a monocle. He walked into the room with poise and an air of pride. As he walked closer, he seemed a tad shorter than his initial posture allowed.

"I believe this is the guy you wanted to see," Joe said.

"Thank you. How are the rest of the guests?" I asked.

"They were fine, but being locked in the manor is starting to make people anxious. I don't know how long they can be kept under control," Joe said.

The thought of public unrest was concerning, so I gestured to the older gentleman to introduce himself.

"I am Henry Woodrow, head butler of Evergreen Manor," the gentleman said with a bow.

I waved my hand at Joe, signaling him to leave.

"So, I take it you know why you are here, Mr. Woodrow?" I asked.

"Yes, the maids told me you are the one currently investigating the death of the late master," he answered.

"Then I'll get right to the point. Where were you at the time of the murder?"

"I was in the ballroom like everyone else until I heard Miss Nikola scream. I tried to make haste. There seemed to be such a fuss that the maids and I tried desperately to calm down the guests."

"You were the one to whisper to Mr. Evergreen before he left the ballroom, weren't you?"

"Yes, that was me."

"What did you tell him?"

"I was reminding him of an appointment scheduled around midnight tonight."

"An appointment with who?"

"I'm afraid even I don't know that," the butler said with a sigh.

"How do you not know?" Zed asked.

"When was the appointment scheduled?" I asked.

"I have the answers to both. This morning started as usual. The master wanted his morning coffee along with the paper like any other morning. However, all that seemed to change after I gave him the letters that arrived."

"What did they say?" I asked.

"Well, most of the letters were the usual, coupons to certain stores, investment offers. Nothing out of the ordinary other than a particular letter. The master went to open it and his expression turned grave. As to what was written in the letter, I couldn't tell you. Nor do I know the sender."

"Do you know what the letter looked like?" I asked.

"I believe it had a yellow color," the butler said.

I took out a familiar envelope from my breast pocket and

held it up to the butler. A bit of shock came over the butler's face.

"Why, that's the letter! You found it?"

"No, I am afraid this letter is something else entirely, but I needed a frame of reference," I said, returning the letter to my pocket.

"I see. Well, that's a pity," Woodrow sighed.

"Do you know anyone that would wish to kill Mr. Evergreen?" I asked.

"A man in Mr. Evergreen's position will always attract both jealousy and praise," Woodrow answered.

That was just another fancy way of saying that anyone who felt slighted by Mr. Evergreen could have done the murder. I felt like I was going in circles trying to find a suspect. Feeling annoyed, I thought, *If I can't find a suspect then I'll have to make one.*

"What happened to the mistress of the house?" I asked.

For a moment, Woodrow was struck with a tinge of melancholy on his face.

"I see. You want to know what happened to Nikola's mother."

I gestured for Woodrow to continue.

"She became ill. She dealt with her ailment for a while before finally succumbing to it. The doctors said she was over-stressed and, of course, the drinking didn't help matters either. Nikola cried a lot that day. Even now, it is apparent that she still misses her mother dearly."

"What was the cause of her stress?" I asked, steepling my hands.

"Well, I suppose since the master is dead and there is no need to keep it a secret now," Woodrow said.

Woodrow coughed slightly as he stared out the window and

gazed at the blizzard raging outside.

"Truth be told, the real reason for Maria Evergreen's death was none other than Alderheim Evergreen himself."

Interlude

Before she met Alderheim, her name was Maria Swan. Henry Woodrow, the butler, went on to explain the life of Nikola's mother, from her origins to her death. Maria didn't come from an exemplary background, quite the contrary, and instead hailed from pretty meager beginnings. She came from a humble family; her mother was a baker and her father served as carpenter and a part-time producer of many shows for newcomers. Her father owned a small-time theater that promoted shows for amateur writers and actors around town. It was through one of her father's shows that Maria discovered her love of dancing, ballet especially. Ever since, she spent almost every waking moment in pursuit of her calling. She practiced rigorously to perfect her skills and capture the audience's gaze wherever she glided onto the stage. Though she started young, her popularity slowly rose and eventually she gained the attention of the public. Before long, she was invited to many high-profile venues to perform, even a few private shows. People sang her praises until eventually she was noticed by the high society set. Not long after, she met Alderheim Evergreen.

Believe it or not, the initial meeting between Alderheim and Maria was not love at first sight. Alderheim partook in one of her shows and found her impressive. Drawn in by Maria, he found himself going to a few more of her shows until he decided to arrange a private event for her to perform at the Manor. Maria accepted, not wanting to miss a chance to increase her popularity. Of course, Alderheim was the only one present to watch her performance but it made no difference to Maria. After her dance, Alderheim tried to express interest in Maria. However, she didn't seem receptive. After all, Maria's real love was with the art of dancing and performing. Romance always seemed like an afterthought to her. Maria knew that if she seriously considered the idea of marriage, her dancing career could end abruptly. Alderheim was disappointed but seemed to respect her decision.

Maria's career took off not long after that, but the good times were short lived. Issues materialized and Maria's parents fell on some difficult times. Her father struggled to find shows to produce, which started to cost the family money. Soon, they were forced to tap into their savings just to keep the theater open. Maria's career took a hit as a result. She continued to do her best to perform where she could, but suddenly not many people seemed to care so much about her shows. A few loyal fans continued to stand by her, but it became obvious that not even the adoration from a few fans could save her career. Luckily, the family bakery was still in good standing, albeit barely. The bakery used to be flooded with many customers dying to catch a glimpse of Maria, but that suddenly shifted to only a few regular patrons a week. With Maria's declining career and her family's desperate struggle for money, all seemed lost. Undeterred, Maria persisted. She'd spent her whole life in pursuit of her dream and she wasn't ready to throw in the towel. The only question left was how.

Alderheim Evergreen lingered throughout the downturn. He heard of the struggles of Maria's family and, sensing Maria's determination, he decided to lend his assistance. Maria had decided to appear for one final show, one that would make all her other old shows pale in comparison. With Maria's expertise on the stage and Alderheim's wealth and connections, such an idea seemed well in the realm of possibilities. Alderheim agreed on one condition and Maria accepted. She'd do whatever she could to help her parents out of poverty. Together, the pair agreed to put on one of the greatest shows ever.

Weeks went into preparation, and Maria made sure to practice even harder than she ever had before. Alderheim was busy securing funding and advertising the show so thoroughly that there wasn't a single person around that wasn't excited about seeing Maria's greatest performance. Finally, on Christmas Day, everyone in town gathered to see the spectacle. From television to radio, almost every type of media was used to capture the show and broadcast it to the world. The show was called *"The Season of Miracles"* And Maria received a tearful standing ovation from many who attended. Many sung Maria's praises for her performance, and they wondered what would be next in her career. However, such a show was truly deserving of a grand finale. The public wasn't aware of it yet, but this was to be Maria's final major show. During production, Maria gave in to Alderheim's advances, and the two had fallen in love. While it might have been a teary farewell, Maria still smiled in front of the audience. Not long after, Maria married Alderheim, and their wedding was the subject of significant press attention. The two of them lived happily ever after.

Chapter VI

Tapping my fingers patiently, I listened and waited for the butler to finish his narrative.

"Are you sure about that?" I asked after hearing Henry's long explanation.

"At least, that was how public opinion interpreted it," responded Henry.

"So how did Alderheim kill his wife?" I asked.

"Simple, he didn't." I raised an eyebrow as Henry continued. "Mr. Evergreen was responsible for her death, but he did not kill Maria, not directly. No, what killed her was her inability to perform."

"You expect me to believe that she died because she wasn't able to dance again?" I asked.

Henry took off his monocle and wiped the glass with a sad and reluctant smile. He returned the monocle to his eye and glared intensely. His gaze caused Zed's ears to perk up with alertness. I returned a look, unfazed.

"You don't seem to understand that we all have our purpose in this world. Some of us were born to serve, some were born to rule," Henry said.

"That's one way of looking at things," Zed responded.

"That's the only way. Take yourselves, for example, you

clearly find meaning in what you are doing in solving this mysterious murder. You didn't run and hide like the rest of the guests, you took charge."

"What's your point?" I asked.

"My point is, some of us just naturally stand above others. Maria was meant to grace the stage and dance. However, that dream was stolen by Mr. Evergreen. Ever since their marriage, Maria was forced to give up her passion to be a lowly housewife."

"What do you mean by 'forced?'" I asked.

The butler released a heavy sigh. "How exactly do you think the late master and Maria ended up married?" Woodrow said.

"Well, according to your story, she seemed very thankful to Alderheim for helping her put on the greatest comeback of her career. My guess is in the process of working on her final show, Alderheim and Maria grew closer and they became more receptive to each other. That opened her up to the prospect of marriage. Am I close?" I asked.

"Seems you got it figured out, detective. Answer this, why did she give up dancing after the marriage?" Woodrow asked.

I paused while trying to figure it out. However, the more I considered Henry's story, the more I realized that it didn't make any sense.

"Maybe she didn't want to be overwhelmed being a house-wife and a dancing superstar?" Zed answered.

"No, if Woodrow is to be believed, then Maria was de-termined to stay on the stage. She firmly believed that performance was her calling. There is no way she would settle for being a housewife. Which makes me wonder..." I explained.

"You really don't know, do you?" Zed and I remained silent

as Henry continued.

"Master Evergreen put a restriction on Maria once they were married. He convinced her to retire from show business. As Maria's career blossomed, so did the attention from many admirers. Apparently, there was a rumor that accused Maria of a scandal. Seduction behind closed doors to boost her career, that sort of thing. Master Evergreen didn't want to be on the receiving end of those rumors."

"He wanted to protect his image so he was willing to dim her star," Zed said.

"He had Maria quit dancing as they got married," I clarified.

"You should've seen her after they got married," said Woodrow. "At first, it seemed to be fine, but after a while you could see how much she missed the stage. Sometimes, when Master Evergreen was away, she would dance just for the sake of dancing. Maria never cared much for high society. Playing the role of the Master's wife, it was as if she was—"

"Living in a dollhouse," I chimed in.

"Why yes. It seems you do understand," Woodrow said.

"But how does this prove Alderheim killed her?" Zed asked.

"The stress of being something she wasn't while being forced to hide what she was. That combination led to some very drastic decisions. Although, things did take a slight turn for the better when she came around."

"Nikola," I said.

"Yes. Nikola was a beautiful child. Ever since her birth, Maria's attitude became cheerful. She enjoyed spending every day with her daughter, especially the holidays when they would practice and dance together for fun."

"Guess she was happy being a stay at home mom after all," Zed remarked.

Henry smiled for a moment as he reminisced. It quickly turned into a grimace as he continued his tale.

"Unfortunately, those happy days didn't last for long. After some time, she and Master Evergreen got into a big argument and eventually the two grew cold and distant. Master Evergreen even considered banishing the mistress from the manor. This was never reported to the public, and on the outside they still appeared to be a happy family. However, behind closed doors, they were anything but."

"How did Nikola cope with all of this?" I asked.

"We, as in the other servers of the Manor, looked after her. Lady Nikola never really saw her parents together anymore. Although, she still visited her mother regularly, which made Maria light up with joy. Sadly, after years of keeping up appearances, the stress of the ordeal led Maria to excessive drinking to cope. What was once a lovely pastime between mother and daughter became a bitter reminder of the past. Naturally, we shielded Nikola from her mother as she drank herself to oblivion. We tried to take good care of Nikola, but nothing could replace her mother's touch. As for Maria, it was only natural that her health would decline. It was a miracle she lasted so long. It was only five years ago that Maria Evergreen finally passed away," Henry explained as a pained expression washed over his face.

Knowing the backstory of the Evergreen family was interesting and eye-opening, but several questions still swam around in my mind.

"Was Alderheim surprised at his wife's passing?" I asked.

"No, not really. Obviously, he took care of and attended the funeral proceedings, in addition to playing the role of a newly widowed husband left alone with his daughter. However, he never shed a tear for her, not even to the public," Henry answered.

"How did Alderheim treat Nikola before and after Maria's passing?" I pressed.

"Master Evergreen didn't seem to mind lady Nikola until that frightful argument he had with Maria. From then on, he distanced himself from her. He tended only to her necessities and left us caretakers to do the rest. Maria was more in control of Nikola's personal development until the stress took over. After Maria's passing, Master Evergreen was forced to take a more direct and strict approach to Lady Nikola."

"When exactly did those rumors about Maria start?"

Henry looked confused, not sure how to answer.

"Uh, well, if memory serves, it happened at the height of Maria's career. That must have been around the time she was doing private shows. Though I don't see how that has—"

"Thanks for your time, Mr. Woodrow. If we need anything else, we'll be sure to come fetch you. For now, can you give us a list of all the guests that attended the party?" I asked.

Henry looked even more confused, but he got up all the same.

"I'll get the list to you as soon as I can," Woodrow said. He bowed and then left the room.

While the Elven butler took his leave, I stared outside the window at the raging winds blowing and howling furiously.

"This'll be a long night."

Chapter VII

I was lost in thought as I stared at the blizzard outside, contemplating the information from Henry Woodrow. Questions swirled in my head. *Who killed Alderheim and why? Does it have something to do with Maria's death? How could she give up everything? And Nikola, Nikola, Nikola. Why, Nikola?*

"KAI!!"

"Huh?" I snapped back to reality.

"Sheesh, Kai I thought I lost you there," Zed said.

"Sorry, I've just been mulling over the details of this case."

"You figure anything out?"

"I said I had a few ideas, but there are many things that are not making too much sense right now."

I kept thinking about the questions in my mind and how to answer them. Not knowing what to do, I paced around Alderheim's office. I searched the office again to see if I may have missed anything.

I considered the maids, Elizabeth and Mary, and thought about the doll's strange behavior. Without knowing exactly why, I decided to reenact the doll's actions during the interview. Sitting down on the chair, I shifted my eyes to the right, mimicking Mary's perspective. At first, I saw nothing but the wall but then I noticed how strange it was to have a potted plant off in the corner. Curious, I investigated. Calling Zed to my side, we both looked at the plant, checking for anything peculiar. An evergreen tree, it was a typical plant for this time of year and a very obvious choice of decor from the late Mr. Evergreen. At first, nothing seemed to be out of the ordinary. Zed sniffed the plant a few times then the pot. After a few moments, Zed worked himself into a fit and started to dig up the dirt.

"You found something?" I asked.

"For some reason, I smell Alderheim's scent in the dirt," Zed answered while covering the carpet with dirt.

I pulled the tree out of the pot as Zed kept digging in the pot. As we dumped the rest of the dirt onto the floor, a key fell out. Zed sniffed it repeatedly.

"Yeah, this key reeks of Evergreen's scent," Zed nodded.

Why was this key hidden and what does it open? Following my train of thought, Zed moved towards the desk in the office. He sniffed around the desk, then began scratching it.

"Something here smells similar to the key," Zed said.

Hearing this, I looked through each drawer of the desk until I noticed a tiny slip of paper sticking out from the corner of the center drawer. The drawer had a keyhole, so I had presumed it to be locked. I attempted to use the key we'd just found, but strangely it didn't fit. Stranger still, the drawer was already unlocked. *Actually*, I noticed, *the lock is broken.* Looking closer, I saw the scratches on the outside of the keyhole and the appearance of something jammed into the hole. *Forced entry.*

Slowly, I opened the drawer and was greeted by a smattering of papers scattered around. Picking my way through the disorder, I combed through the papers. Zed reverted back to human form to help me sift through the papers. Each one was a handwritten letter. The contents of the letters ranged from business updates to clandestine meetings. Surprisingly, some letters were written with a sense of urgency. The contents of the letters started off with a simple retelling of the person's day until they shifted in tone and content. They didn't go into explicit detail, but the youthful vigor of the first batch of letters morphed in a more mangled and confusing dialogue. Whoever wrote those letters was clearly 'fed up' and didn't know what to do. The last letter, posted three days ago, was the most troubling. "Help me." That was the extent of it. Nothing else that came after it.

"I wonder what they needed help with," Zed said with trepidation.

"Good question," I said.

I scrutinized the letters, searching for any commonality among them. I scoured the first threatening letter I had received, along with the second letter that had been discovered in the late Mr. Evergreen. Unfortunately, I couldn't find anything in common between the letters I'd received and the ones found in Mr. Evergreen's desk. The handwriting was completely different and the texture of the papers also differed. When I turned the letters over, I noticed an important detail.

"Zed, turn over the letters and check the address."

When he did, it was apparent that the recipient address of some of the letters found in the desk was the same as the sender's address for the threatening letter I received in the morning.

The pieces are starting to fall into place, I thought.

Zed, still surprised at our recent discovery, continued to rummage through the desk. Meanwhile, I scanned the documents and tried to find out what I could about either the sender or the recipients. I was knee-deep in paperwork when Zed caught my attention.

"Kai, I think you ought to see this."

"What is it?" I asked, keeping my attention on documents.

"On March 1, Mr. Evergreen appeared to have a meeting with the Vanholt family," Zed recited.

"How do you know that?"

"Here," Zed said and then he presented me with a small black book with an Evergreen symbol on the cover. Intrigued, I began flipping through Mr. Evergreen's appointment book. The records for all of his appointments spanned from years back. Without wasting any time, I promptly skipped to his latest recorded meeting.

According to Woodrow, it should've been the morning of December 24.

Nothing was there. Instead, the final entry was on December 22. I couldn't find anything after, including absolutely nothing indicating a meeting on the 24th. I entertained the possibility that Woodrow had lied to me, until I noticed a trace of a small piece of paper in the spine of the book.

No doubt, these pages have been ripped out.

"Zed, where did you find this?" I asked.

"It was in the same drawer that we found all those letters. I almost didn't notice it beneath all the papers covering the book," Zed answered while pointing at the drawer.

"But it's strange," Zed continued.

"What is?"

"Well, it's just that I thought we would get a lot more letters than just these."

"What do you mean?"

"When you opened the drawer, it looked like there were a lot of papers were crammed in. After taking them all out, it looks like the letters don't amount to much."

I paused for a moment to consider Zed's words. However, before I addressed Zed's observation, I passed him one of the many letters in Mr. Evergreen's desk.

"Sniff this and tell me what do you make of it."

Zed took a whiff of the letter in an exaggerated fashion. When he was satisfied, he returned to the letter in a confident manner.

"Besides the scentless ink, the letter has Alderheim's scent on it along with a side of milk and cookies."

I narrowed my eyes. "Did you say milk?" I asked sternly.

Zed shrank at the slight change in my voice. "Y-yeah, that's important?"

I held the book to Zed's nose. He instinctively inhaled the black book.

"And?" I asked.

"Well, for starters, the book reeks of Mr. Evergreen," Zed said while waving his hand over his nose.

"What else?"

"The only other thing I got out of this is—"

"Milk and cookies?"

"Pretty much."

"Interesting. So that's how it is."

I stroked my chin as I paced around the desk. Zed stared at me, puzzled. Nonetheless, I ignored him and examined the now empty drawer. I put my hand inside, touching the base of the drawer. I knocked on the base and it felt hollow. I looked at the four corners of the drawer while placing both hands inside, hoping for something to grab onto, but found nothing.

After a few minutes, I got on all fours and checked underneath the desk. I felt around the edges of the desk, trying to find an access point. Zed, still standing, was confused as to why our roles had reversed.

"Uh, Kai, I know this might seem odd coming from me, but why are you on all fours rummaging underneath the desk?" Zed asked.

"Because this desk appears to be custom-made and something you mentioned about the number of letters we found bothers me."

What bothered me was how a businessman like Mr. Evergreen would leave a drawer with seemingly important documents so disheveled, to say nothing of the broken lock on the drawer. Plus, Evergreen's black book has pages ripped out of it which should've contained a record of his appointment that night. *The culprit broke into the desk looking for something.*

I kept searching around the desk as I explained my deductions to Zed. On my back, I looked up at the bottom of the drawer, took out my knife, and jostled it at the base of the drawer.

Still puzzled by my actions, Zed asked, "I can understand you believing the culprit broke into the desk, but why are you so sure they didn't just want to rip out those pages from the black book? Theoretically, that's the only piece of evidence tying them to the murder."

Before I could answer Zed's question, a soft popping sound came from inside the drawer itself.

"That's why," I said triumphantly. Zed and I both looked inside the drawer and saw the false bottom.

"After you mentioned there were fewer letters than it originally appeared, I figured that the drawer had a false bottom," I explained.

"But how did you figure the culprit was after whatever is in the false bottom?" Zed asked.

"Alderheim Evergreen is a businessman. There is no way he would keep his desk so untidy, especially since he had a black book containing all of his appointments. I'd wager that when the culprit opened the drawer, the inside was neat and orderly, which would mean that the false bottom didn't become apparent to them as they rummaged through all the documents."

"But what were they looking for?"

"Only one way to find out," I said as I removed the false bottom to find a black folder hidden inside with a peculiar design.

"What's that, a crane or something?" Zed asked.

"Right now, I'm more interested in what's inside." I said.

Zed and I braced ourselves for what we may find inside the folder.

"Huh?" we said in unison.

Inside were two blank pieces of paper. Dumbfounded, I gazed at them, trying to see if there was anything I was missing. I looked at the papers front to back, hoping something would jump out at me. I held the papers upside down and tried a magnifying glass to see if I could find some hidden writing or any marks that could possibly explain the significance of the blank pieces of paper before me. After a while of continuous searching, I decided to give up for the moment.

"Seems like the culprit managed to take what was in the folder," Zed spoke.

"Unlikely. The inside of the drawer showed no signs of forced entry from the false bottom," I corrected.

"But the lock was already busted from the outside. Maybe they used a pen or something to get inside the false bottom and left that intact so we would never notice what they were really after."

Zed's argument was hard to refute. However, I was certain that the culprit didn't know about the false bottom or the folder.

"Let's put our theories to the test," I said, beckoning Zed to come closer.

He approached me nonchalantly and I presented him with the piece of paper for him to smell. Zed complied.

"What do you make of that?" I asked.

He winced slightly as he sniffed. I raised an eyebrow.

"You alright?" I asked.

"Yeah, fine. That paper has some good mileage on it," Zed answered, rubbing his nose.

"What do you mean?"

"For starters, this paper has a strong scent, some of which is from Mr. Evergreen."

"And?"

"There are a bunch of other scents that I haven't experienced before, so I can't really describe them."

"And?"

"One of the minor scents seems to share a bit in common with the key we picked up from the flower pot."

"Interesting, and?"

"And what? I told you all that I got from the paper."

"Are you sure?"

"Yes."

"Positive?"

"YES! What, are you doubting me now?"

"No, quite the contrary. I have one hundred percent faith in your sense of smell," I declared.

"Then what?" Zed asked.

"It's because of that heightened nose of yours that I can say with certainty that this paper is the genuine article. Now, if could only figure out what it is."

"How are you so sure? Because it has Mr. Evergreen's scent? That paper could've come from anywhere maybe the office or—"

"Answer this: why didn't you smell the cookies on the paper?"

This time Zed raised an eyebrow.

"What does that have to do with anything?" Zed asked.

"I just find it strange that you managed to catch a whiff of milk and cookies from the letter and this black book but this piece of paper seems to be free of that scent. How does that happen?" I mused.

"Because the cookies were eaten!" Zed finally realized. "So then that would mean,"

"Go on," I encouraged Zed.

"The reason the letters and the black book have that scent could be because someone ate the milk and cookies while they went through the drawer or immediately before."

I nodded my head in agreement while Zed continued.

"However, it couldn't have been Mr. Evergreen because Nikola told you he didn't like sweets, right?"

"Exactly, and just to make sure, I questioned the maids as well and they also confirmed Nikola's statement. So, if Mr. Evergreen didn't eat the cookies then it must've been—"

"Whoever else broke into the drawer! And because that blank paper lacks the scent of cookies—"

"The culprit never got his hands on this thing. Whatever it may be," I finished.

This line of thinking seemed to be the most plausible. My theory was able to explain the supposed state of the crime scene and what may have transpired after the murder. However, there were still a few things that bothered me. Some things about the case were not explained.

"Why did Mr. Evergreen write all these letters?" Zed asked, casting a glance at them.

"What are you talking about?"

"These letters. I'm wondering why Mr. Evergreen wrote so many but never sent them."

"That's because Evergreen never wrote these letters." I answered.

Zed paused, then scratched his head incredulously. "That doesn't make any sense," Zed said.

"Of course it does," I pulled out the black book and pointed to the pages then continued.

"See how the handwriting in the book is different from the letter? The handwriting in the book is calmer and more business-like, which was fitting for Alderheim Evergreen. However, if we look at the letters, we see—"

"That's not what I meant," Zed interrupted, handing me a piece of paper.

"What doesn't make sense is that if Evergreen didn't write all these, then why did he have all of them?"

The question had me stumped. I took a look at the black folder with the blank piece of paper once more.

"Zed, you mentioned that this paper has a similar scent to the key, correct?"

"Yeah. So?"

"Is it possible for you to find exactly where this key opens?"

"It could lead me to where the key was last used or to another body. You think it could lead us to the culprit?"

"I'm not so sure about that, but I feel as if this key may explain some of the missing links in the case."

"While I try to find what the key opens, what are you gonna do?"

I flashed the black book at Zed. "I'm going to catch up on some much-required reading."

After a brief make-shift salute from Zed, he changed back into a hound as he left the room searching for the next lead. Meanwhile, I decided to sit at the desk and begin to flip through the pages of Alderheim's black book.

"What were you hiding?" I muttered.

Chapter VIII

Half an hour had passed since Zed had left to search the manor for what the mysterious key opened. Meanwhile, I was reading through the black book and trying to make sense of it, or at least narrow down the list of potential suspects by cross-referencing the names in his planner with the party's guest list. So far, the names seemed to match up. However, I noticed one entry that didn't have a name. Instead, there was a strange symbol. Next to it was the word *Livecorp*. There was a series of numbers next to the symbol that showed a pattern of the same transaction once every month. I stared so hard at the pages that my vision blurred. I yawned and rubbed my eyes. It was either very late or very early. Despite the time, my mind was still hard at work. Unfortunately, the more I read and compared names, the less it seemed like I was going anywhere. Even the stupid Warthog was in Evergreen's book for having some kind of loan. The monotony of the schedules began to change when I turned the page.

"Huh?"

For some reason, these pages were filled with notes about trips, both local and abroad, that had been taken in rapid succession. I was quick to dismiss this as a typical business schedule until I noticed that these appointments were longer than his usual hour. During this time, he was meeting with people for two hours or longer. The dates of these meetings seemed a bit sporadic, as well. Turning the page again revealed another interesting nugget.

Maria Swan - 5pm-7:30pm

A knock on the door pulled my attention from the book. I wasn't sure who was knocking, but I could rule out Zed, who would have barged straight in.

"Who is it?" I asked.

"It's me, sugar," the voice said.

"Come in," I said with a grimace.

"Hiya, sugar," said Elizabeth. She was carrying something in her hands.

"Elizabeth, how did you get here?"

"You mean how did I get past that handsome Mr. Turner? Oh, just looking at him can be a treat," Elizabeth said, blushing.

"I told him I had something for you and he let me through without much fuss."

"Okay, so what do you have for me?" I asked.

"Just a good, strong cup of coffee."

She twirled around as she spoke and then presented me with a steaming cup.

"Since you're up burning the midnight oil, the least we can do is offer you something to keep you up," Elizabeth explained.

"Thanks" I said, accepting the cup.

I was apprehensive at first, but after a sip my eyes widened. "Wow, this is pretty good."

"Of course it is. Mr. Evergreen imported some of the best coffee in the world. Or rather, he used to," Elizabeth said.

"Kai," she continued.

I turned to see her rectangular pupils peering at me.

"Do you have any idea who did this?" she asked.

I held her gaze for a moment as I closed the black book.

"Nope. Not really," I said, sipping the coffee.

I wasn't lying. I didn't know who I could point the finger at for Alderheim's murder, not yet, at least. I had some ideas, but there was no way I was going to reveal that to a potential suspect. Elizabeth was unable to hide her disappointment at my answer, and her head lowered.

"Aren't you some master detective? Don't you guys solve stuff like this in like thirty minutes?" Elizabeth asked.

"You watch way too many crime dramas," I said.

Not satisfied, Elizabeth glanced at the desk and found the guest list I was using.

"Why do you have the guest list? Ah! Don't tell me, you suspect one of the guests killed Mr. Evergreen."

"Something like that. I'm using it in a process of elimination," I answered.

"Well, from the number of names crossed off this list, you're running low on suspects," Elizabeth said, as she inched closer to me.

"That's one way to look at it," I answered patiently.

Elizabeth went on talking, but I paid little attention. She was quickly becoming a nuisance, so I did my best to ignore her. That's when an idea came to me.

"Elizabeth, I need your help," I confessed.

"Really? What do you need?" Elizabeth asked.

"As you can see, I've managed to narrow down the list of the guests. I assume you've catered to all the people on this list?"

"Yep."

"I was wondering if you could tell me exactly what they were doing and how they behaved during the party."

"You got it, sugar. So, this guy here was…"

Elizabeth remarked on each of the remaining guests on the list, often droning on in painful detail. I tried my best to feign intrigue as she spoke. The more she explained, the more I wondered how she was able to do her job while also attending to this level of gossip. Eventually, Elizabeth finished her long narration.

"I see, very detailed," I said.

"Was that any help, sugar?"

To Elizabeth's credit, she seemed to have a decent grasp of the guest list. Not that this was especially useful. "Where are the guests now?" I asked.

"They are still in the ballroom, frustrated and scared by the murder. Many have complained, but Mr. Turner is managing to keep the people quiet, for now."

Hmm, I better solve this quickly.

"Without the master of the house, it's a little hard to organize. Sugar, if this keeps up any longer, we may have to put the people in the guest rooms," Elizabeth continued.

That might be a bad idea. "How is Nikola holding up?" I asked.

"You're still worried about her?" Elizabeth teased.

I remained silent, still enjoying my cup of coffee. Elizabeth took the hint and answered without any additional teasing.

"She was shaken up at first, but she's managing to hold herself together. She's helping Woodrow, Mary, and the rest to tend to the guests in the ballroom," Elizabeth explained.

"At least you have the heiress of Evergreen Manor to help ease the workload," I said.

"Hopefully that continues to be the case," Elizabeth whispered.

"What do you mean?"

"Well, regardless of how this murder is resolved, the business side of Mr. Evergreen's investments may not be able to continue without him."

"I'm confused. Wouldn't Nikola, Evergreen's only child, inherit everything?"

"I wonder about that."

"You know something, don't you?" I asked.

Elizabeth was silent and wore a complicated look on her face. I continued to press for answers until Elizabeth eventually relented.

"I assume you've realized there was a bit of a rift between Nikola and her father," Elizabeth said.

I nodded.

"Then you should also know that during my time here Nikola has never seemed interested in taking over her father's business interests. In all honesty, she seemed to vehemently oppose him. I never understood why. When I asked Woodrow about it, he mentioned that their situation used to be a million times worse. That was before I signed on to work with them."

"In other words, due to the turbulent relationship between them, Nikola may not be entitled to anything," I surmised.

"That's assuming she ever had a choice."

"Huh?"

"It's true Nikola would try to oppose her father. However, the longer I've worked here, I began to notice that Evergreen always knew exactly how to get Nikola to behave."

I slowly gulped the coffee and thought back to my first meeting with Nikola.

"How did he do that?" I asked.

"I have no idea. I've been curious about that as well. Nothing has ever seemed out of the ordinary. Most of us just wrote their relationship off as a spoiled trust fund baby going against her father, but…" Elizabeth paused.

My ears perked up, listening intently as Elizabeth continued.

"Even though I may not have worked here as long as Woodrow has, I can't help but feel that it's all wrong. I've heard a lot of whispers calling Nikola 'an ice queen' or 'the spoiled heiress.' The list of nicknames goes on and on."

"So? People love to spread that kind of gossip. Being rich and famous only exacerbates the issue," I said nonchalantly.

Elizabeth bit her lip and glared at me.

"Would someone who was considered an ice queen show concern for those working under her? Would she try to befriend her own maids? Would she be capable of having a smile that could light up the room? Would someone so spoiled go out of their way to defy their wealthy father?"

To my surprise, tears welled up in Elizabeth's eyes.

"Nobody has ever bothered to try to understand her. She isn't some heartless, greedy rich kid. Nikola is a girl that lost her mother at a young age and was stuck with an aggressive and controlling father as her only means for support. Nobody seems to understand that. Nobody sees how she retreats to her room and ducks away from the pressures of keeping up appearances. She still tries to cling to some semblance of happiness, but nobody sees that side of her. All they see is a spoiled kid going against her seemingly benevolent father. Now that father is dead and she's all alone with no one else to turn to," Elizabeth explained.

The maid was staring daggers at me. I remained speechless at the sight of her angry, teary-eyed face. I took a moment to properly register Elizabeth's words and recall my brief encounter with Nikola.

"I never condoned how people treated Nikola. I was just pointing to an unfortunate fact of human nature," I said and then gulped down the remaining lukewarm coffee. "My job is to find the truth in whatever form it takes, regardless of any sob story."

Elizabeth looked like she had more to say, but before she could question me further the door swung open. Zed looked to be in a bit of a panic. Elizabeth frantically wiped away her tears and tried to regain a smile.

"Am I interrupting something?" Zed asked.

"Not at all. I was just leaving," Elizabeth said. Then she gathered both our mugs and headed for the door. As she left, Elizabeth waved her hands and said, "Good luck. Find the truth."

"What was that about?" Zed asked.

"Nothing too important. Have you found anything?" I asked.

"After great effort, I believe I found the door we were looking for. Obviously, it was locked."

"Excellent. Hopefully, this brings us one step closer to finding the truth," I said.

I grabbed the book and other pieces of evidence as Zed and I prepared our exit. As we were leaving, a fleeting thought crept into my mind. *I just hope this is a truth everyone can accept.*

Walking along the long hallway to the door he'd found, Zed morphed into his hound form and put his nose to the ground. Meanwhile, my nose was in the black book. I was still trying to make sense of the date and times within. My head was swirling with all the evidence and testimonies I'd gathered, though. I was still far from having a complete picture of the case. There were still so many unanswered questions, and I hoped that Zed's new discovery would lead to the final answers we were lacking.

"Why'd you make Elizabeth cry?" Zed asked.

"You heard us?"

"Not really, I just smelled her fear and sadness from behind the door and was curious about what happened."

The image of Elizabeth's teary-eyed face was still vivid in my mind.

"I was just given a new perspective on things," I answered.

As we walked, I told Zed about Elizabeth giving me details on the guests at the party that coincided with the names in the black book. We walked down a flight of stairs while discussing the case.

"Did Elizabeth help you to find our culprit?" asked Zed.

"More like she helped me to eliminate most of the suspects," I replied.

I wasn't sure where Zed was leading me, but I couldn't help but notice that the overall aesthetic of the Manor had shifted over the course of our trip. The ballroom had a Gothic theme, including a couple of mosaics of demons chasing angels. However, as Zed and I went deeper in the manor, I noticed some changes. While the rest of the Manor still retained its Gothic style, the presence of demon imagery became more apparent. The angels from before seemed to slowly fade away as we traversed the castle. After a while, Zed came to a stop and pointed at a door.

"There it is," Zed declared.

The door itself was made of wood and didn't appear to be special at all. At the foot of the door was a tattered floor mat that had writing on it, but the mat was too scratched up to read. On either side of the door were two identical suits of armor, each held an axe.

"You sure this is the door the key is supposed to open?" I asked.

"Having doubts?" Zed replied.

"The door seems a bit flimsy. I can't imagine why someone would put so much effort into hiding the key when you could easily break it down," I said, casually walking towards it with the key in my hand.

"Seems that way but—wait!" Zed shouted.

Too late.

As I stood in front of the door, I felt the ground shift beneath me. A symbol glowed beneath my feet. As I tried to assess the sudden change, the two suits of armor sprang to life. Both turned in my direction, their axes poised to come down on top of me. Realizing I sprung some kind of trap, I plunged the key into the keyhole and turned the lock. With the door opened, Zed sped past like a guided missile, knocking me into the room with a tumble. Both of the axes stopped mid-swing when I was shoved off the pressure mechanism. When the suits of armor rotated back into their original positions, Zed and I breathed.

"I was trying to tell you to 'watch your step' like the mat said. I smelled a trace of mana," Zed groaned.

I turned to look at the floor mat behind us. Sure enough, the words 'watch your step' were barely visible through the tattered claw marks.

"How did you know what the mat said? I could barely read it at all," I asked.

"Because when I first found the door I smelled traces of mana. But I was too late and accidentally triggered the ward.

Luckily, I was able to avoid it," Zed answered.

"Next time start with that explanation, please and thank you!" I complained.

"Next time wait for me to finish my explanation," Zed rebuked.

"Looks like the trap was designed to stop a human and you lucked out and avoided the trap while you were on four legs," I explained.

"Yet the great detective couldn't see the evidence of the trap by himself." Zed mocked.

Inside the room, we were greeted by a rug made from an enormous polar bear. Along the walls were trophies of deer, moose, foxes, and wolves. Zed shuddered at the sight of wolf heads on the walls. The room itself had seemed to go on forever, with plenty of animal paraphernalia to compliment the dark aesthetic. Given the state of the room, I figured it would be difficult to find anything particularly unusual. As I walked further, I couldn't help but remark, "Mr. Evergreen sure loved putting his trophies on display."

The more I observed, I noticed a subtle shift in the decor. Yes, there were still animal trophies around, there also were a few paintings on the walls. They looked expensive and ranged from realism to expressionism. Due to the extensive size of the area, Zed and I agreed to split up, hoping to find anything out of the ordinary.

I stopped to admire the paintings for a minute. I was hoping that maybe they could give me a clue about this room. I wasn't sure if there was a secret passageway or a hidden treasure here, but I was certain that the room was booby-trapped for a reason and that the key had been hard to find.

"I just need something to connect the dots. Anything," I said.

As if responding to my cry, I heard a loud crash from Zed's direction. I turned and readied my knife for any would-be attacker. All I could see was that Zed had tumbled onto the floor.

"Ow," Zed groaned.

It appeared that he had tripped over a brass candelabra on the floor.

"What happened?" I asked.

"Some bear was about to fall on top of me," Zed said, pointing to the collapsed stuffed bear in front of him.

"The stuffed animal startled you and you slipped on this candelabra?" I affirmed.

"I was just trying to avoid the stuffed bear till that thing tripped me up."

"You okay?" I said, helping him up and ignoring his makeshift bravado.

"Yeah. I was following the scent, trying to find my way around."

"You found the scent? Where?"

"Just around the corner over there." Zed pointed.

I followed his finger to a corridor around the corner of the room. Zed regained his composure and took the lead as I followed behind. The further we walked, the more I noticed how many items were scattered on the floor, from pillows to wilted flowers. When we finally made it out of the corridor, we were greeted by more paintings. Unlike the ones from before, these were portraits. Zed went to the left of the room while my attention remained focused on the center. On the wall was a portrait of Alderheim Evergreen and Nikola. Alderheim appeared simultaneously happy and stern, while Nikola wore a modest smile on her face. I wasn't fooled by it. After spending the night with her at the party, it became very apparent to me that her modest smile was nothing but a facade to appease her father. The eyes are the window to the soul, and they reveal our true intentions. I turned my attention to another portrait and noticed something strange about it. It was a portrait a young woman with a broad stroke of green across her eyes, making her identity appear anonymous.

"But even with the broad stroke, it is clear to see—"

"Kai! You may wanna check this out," Zed called to me. Curious, I walked towards the sound of his voice.

As I walked towards him, I noticed a picture frame on the floor. I picked up the facedown photo and saw that the glass had been smashed. Among the shards was a picture of the Evergreen family from long ago. A much younger Nikola stood innocently in the middle. The smile on her face was a lot more innocent and genuine in the picture. Alderheim's hair only had a few streaks of gray and he stood next to a beautiful woman who was smiling despite her tired-looking eyes. I gazed at the picture until I noticed another picture of the family. This one had drastic differences from the first. In the second picture, Alderheim had a bit more gray in his hair and Nikola was a bit older. She was smiling, but this one seemed plastic, as if she was posing to maintain the status quo. The woman, however, had no such pretext. Her demeanor was one of cold seriousness.

"What happened?" I said.

I continued to move forward. The further I walked, the more pictures I saw. It was as if I was walking backwards in time and seeing the origins of the Evergreen family. The long hallway was filled with plenty of pictures. Some were hanging crookedly, while others were smashed to bits on the wall. The next picture I saw was of a much younger Alderheim with a full head of black hair standing next to the silver-haired woman. It looked to be their wedding day. Alderheim had a satisfied smile on his face, while the woman had a gentle smile on her face. Something about that gentle smile seemed off, as if she were a bird resigned to her cage. I couldn't help but shake the feeling of foreboding. I finally reached a door at the end of the hall. It had been left slightly ajar. I opened the door fully to let myself in and what I saw was truly unexpected.

"This- This is…!"

Chapter IX

So much for a simple holiday. We were smack dab in the middle of yet another case. Who else but the 'great detective Kai' would take on a case on Christmas? Give me a break. Alderheim Evergreen, the host of that big Christmas party, was murdered. So obviously, it was up to us to figure it out. 'How?' you ask. Good question. You'd think in order to solve such a murder we would be interrogating every suspect. However, things never go that simply. Instead, we were walking around investigating a trophy room of sorts. There were plenty of animal pelts. Bears, foxes, wolves—you name it and, chances are, Alderheim probably hunted it and placed them somewhere in that room. The sight of these stuffed animals and the mounts on the wall was enough to make me shudder. It may have been my beast half-mourning the loss of fallen comrades. Ah, where are my manners? The name is Zed, Detective Kai's partner. I'm sure you have some questions, like what happened to the previous narrator? Well, that man can never sit still for long, so I've been entrusted with giving my account of this tale.

Kai and I wandered around the room with dead animals that seemed to go on forever. Honestly, I wasn't entirely sure what we were supposed to look for. I glanced back at

Kai, who seemed to be deep in thought while he scanned the room. Chances are he didn't know what to look for either. For some reason, the room's style seemed to change bit by bit the more we traversed deeper inside. I had no idea why the room changed from the gallery of the most dangerous creatures to a random art gallery. Then I noticed a change in Kai's expression. He must've been puzzled by the change in design as well. It seemed so abrupt, not to mention how the designs clashed with each other.

"Zed," Kai called.

I looked up at him, waiting for his response. His gaze was fixed on the paintings in front of him.

"This room seems a bit bigger than normal, so—"

"You want us to split up and cover more ground?" I finished.

"I call dibs on the art gallery side. You can deal with all the animal trophies." Kai smirked at me.

He knew how the other side of the room made me feel a bit uneasy. He can be a bit of a jerk at times. Not wanting to argue, I decided to shrug my shoulders, get back on all fours, and start sniffing around. Kai turned back around, staring intently at the painting. It was pretty clear to me that neither of us knew exactly what we were looking for in that room. However, my superior sense of smell gave me a slight edge over Kai. See, ever since we found that key in Alderheim's study, I was able to use the scent to back track all the way to the trophy room. I could still smell the scent of the key in the room, although that led to a problem: I could still smell the scent everywhere. Apparently, Alderheim loved frequenting this room, so practically everything had his scent. "This is going to be annoying," I said.

After searching for a while, neither of us had the slightest idea of what we were looking for. I could tell Kai hadn't found anything either, as he would have made it known by now if he had. Honestly, I wasn't sure if this room even had anything to do with the murder at all. However, I knew Kai wasn't ready to throw in the towel yet, which meant I would have no choice but to keep searching until we both exhausted every possibility. I just continued to walk along, investigating every nook and cranny I could find.

I walked with my nose to the ground, hoping to find something of note, when I found a candelabra in the middle of the floor. It looked like someone had dropped it. Curious, I took a few sniffs. Once I was convinced the candelabra had nothing to do with our case, I tried to proceed forward until I bumped my head onto something big. I looked up and saw a giant bear ready to lunge at me. The bear tried to collapse on top of me, but I immediately jumped back to avoid the creature. Unfortunately, when I jumped back, I landed on the candelabra and I lost my footing and fell. I let out a yip which was followed by a loud thud. Admittedly, it wasn't my most graceful moment. Before I could react to the seething pain in the back of my head, Kai appeared above me with a knife in hand.

"What the heck happened?" Kai asked with concern.

"Some random bear was about to lunge at me," I explained.

"You mean one of the dozens of stuffed bears in this place?"

"Yeah. It was just in front of me," I said and pointed.

Kai followed my paw. His face went from concern to annoyance.

"You got scared and, in an effort, to get away you slipped on this?" Kai said picking up a candelabra from off the ground.

"Who said I was scared? I was just trying to avoid the stupid thing," I argued.

"Yeah, yeah. Are you alright?" Kai asked, offering a hand.

"I'm just peachy," I said, accepting Kai's help.

"I was busy following another scent but—"

"You found another scent? Where?"

I pointed in the direction I was going. Kai clapped his hands twice in excitement. "Well, lead the way."

Since Kai had started to follow me, being around the "trophies" became a little bit more bearable. We soon passed through a corridor.

"Why is this place so big?" I asked.

"Not sure, but with a place this big we are bound to find whatever Evergreen was trying to hide."

As we traversed the corridor, was saw a few items scattered across the floor. They made no difference to me at the time, as I was merely following the scent I was tracking, but when I turned back to check on Kai, I would see him examining the items. He never stopped to look, but he would glance at them as if they held some kind of significance. After a while, we came out of the corridor to a vast art gallery.

"Did we just make one giant circle?" I asked.

"No," Kai said while casting a serious gaze toward the center of the room.

I looked ahead to a portrait of Alderheim Evergreen and Nikola. Kai approached the portrait, lost in thought. However, I didn't care enough to look at paintings all night. Besides, I still had the scent to follow.

"I'll be going on ahead," I reported to Kai.

He wordlessly raised his hand, signaling to me that he will catch up.

I left Kai to ponder and found another hallway. The hallway

was completely dark and it was virtually impossible to see anything.

"Give me a break," I said.

It would be impossible for anyone except me since my eyes can see in the dark. The hallway seemed to go on for a long while. There was a lot of broken glass and picture frames across the floor. It was annoying having to avoid the glass while walking on all fours. Eventually, I reached the end and it seemed to be devoid of light as well. However, I spotted a long candle fuse. Eager to light the place up, I unsheathed my claws and swiped at the stone wall near the fuse. The sparks from my claws ignited the fuse. This caused a chain reaction that making all the candles in the room to light up one after another. Soon, the whole place was lit up, including the hallway leading to the room. When the area became fully illuminated, I took another good look around the room. The place seemed like it accumulated a lot of dust over the years.

"What a mess," I said.

However, it wasn't just the dust, the entire room seemed to be in shambles. The room looked as if a typhoon had hit it. Many unlit candles were scattered on the floor along with decorative drapes that were ripped up in various places. There was so much broken glass from multiple vases and picture frames. I gingerly walked past the shards as I made my way to the center of the room. Walking along the path of destruction, I made it to the center to be greeted by a single portrait on the wall surrounded by ripped up drapes. A candelabra was tossed on the floor in front of the portrait along with some cushions that had been thrown about. A few crimson stains near the picture managed to catch my attention. Thinking the worst, I decided to take a whiff of the stains along the floor. It smelled like merlot, which put me at ease.

"For a second, I almost thought Kai and I had to solve two murders," I said.

I honestly had no idea what to make of the room itself, so I turned my attention to the portrait. In it was a very beautiful young woman with white, silverish hair and a gentle yet charming smile.

"Is that a picture of Nikola?" I asked.

I stared hard at the picture as if trying to uncover its secrets. I tried to put myself in the mind of Kai to see what I can glean from this room. However, no matter how hard I tried, I couldn't figure it out. *Kai makes this stuff look so easy,* I thought.

Faced with no other options, I decided to call the man himself.

"Kai! You may wanna see this."

After a few minutes, Kai came running through the corridor until he stopped to take in all of the surroundings. He walked towards me carefully, paying attention to the mess that was strewn around the room.

"It looks like a typhoon hit this place," I said.

"An angry one," Kai corrected.

What kind of typhoon gets angry? I thought.

"I thought this painting looked familiar. What do you make of it?" I said, pointing to the portrait in the center of the room.

At first, Kai stared into the painting with confusion. Suddenly, Kai's expression changed from confusion to consternation. His actions became untamed as he frantically looked around the room. This was different from his previous behavior, as he was looking around the room with more vigor and purpose.

"Kai, what's the matter with you? You're starting to act like me when I'm looking for my favorite bone," I said.

Kai paid no heed to me as he continued to look around. He found the wine stain I discovered earlier and lingered there for a while.

"This is wine, right?" Kai asked.

"How'd you guess?"

"Not all of the glass came from the broken picture frames, some looked to have come from a wine glass. Besides, if it was blood, I'd imagine there would be more of it, considering the state of the room. Also, you and I should both know the smell of blood by now and this doesn't smell like it," Kai explained.

"Then what's so important about the stain?" I asked.

"Nothing."

"What?" I blinked.

Kai smirked at my reaction.

"What is important is how the stain got here," Kai said and then dusted off his hands in satisfaction. "Well, I believe we've seen quite enough of this place." Kai began to leave the room, so I followed behind. I tried to get Kai to explain what he meant. Unfortunately, my questions fell on deaf ears as Kai walked up the stairs. I bumped into his back as he stood in place, checking his watch.

"It's getting late. We need to wrap up this case quickly," Kai said, still checking his watch.

"If we walk all the way back to the office it'll take about fifteen minutes," I said.

"Good thing we got a shortcut," Kai said with a snap of his fingers.

Back in the office, Kai sat at the desk with his feet up. He placed a few things on the desk, such as Alderheim's black book and all of the letters we had received. Kai kept staring up at the ceiling like he was waiting for something. I had no idea what was going on in his head, but I decided to spend some time thinking about the case and how it had proceeded so far. Obviously, the most suspicious person was Nikola, as she mysteriously left the ballroom and was left alone with her father for an unknown amount of time. The only thing I was thinking was how would we be able to prove how she killed him and get her to confess. Then there was a knock on the door, and Joe barged in without waiting for our response.

"Huh? I thought you guys were out," Joe said.

"We were. Then we took the express way back," Kai mused.

"In any case, the people in the ballroom are becoming unruly. We may have a riot on our hands soon."

Kai casually looked at his watch and closed his eyes. After a big sigh, he opened his eyes with firm resolution.

"Alright, let's not keep the people waiting any longer," Kai said flippantly.

"Have you figured everything out?" Joe asked.

"More or less. There are a few things I have to confirm first."

"Such as?" I chimed in.

"Spoilers, my dear Zed," Kai answered.

"Wait, so you really know who did it?" I asked, shocked.

Kai loves to save these moments for a big reveal. The glint in Kai's eyes was unmistakable.

"Joe, I need you to bring me…"

Chapter X

While the first suspect didn't surprise me at all, the second suspect had me puzzled. I laid down on the ground as a hound and waited for the people to arrive. Kai was patiently sitting at the desk as he twirled a knife in his hand. I remained on the floor and stared at the door, still trying to understand what Kai was thinking. Despite all of our work together, I still didn't have an idea of what was going on in that skull of his. He had the annoying habit of being so secretive and not wanting to reveal the cards in his hand. I was used to it, but it didn't make it any less annoying.

Still wracking my brain about the case, I heard snoring.

"What the?"

Confused, I turned to see Kai casually taking a nap on the desk. Surprised, with my mouth hung open, I sprung to my feet.

"Oi, wake up!" I yelled.

Kai opened one eye. After looking around, he stretched his body and an enormous yawn escaped his mouth. He rubbed his eyes. It amazed me how casual Kai was, given the circumstances.

"Hmm? Are we under attack?" he asked.

"No."

"Did the guest arrive?"

"No."

"Then what's the issue?"

"Why are you asleep?"

"I thought it would help me figure out who the culprit is."

My jaw dropped at the absurd comment. "Kai, I'm serious."

"So was I. Besides, we've been up all night. I thought getting a bit of shut-eye could do some good. We may be in for more at this rate," Kai said.

Before I could argue, there was a knock on the door.

"Come in," Kai said.

Joe walked into the room with two others following behind. Joe cleared his throat.

"I brought Nikola Evergreen and Henry Woodrow, just like you asked."

"Very good, Mr. Turner. Oh, and Joe, be sure to keep an eye on the guest in the ballroom." Kai winked.

Joe raised an eyebrow but did as he was told, departing the room and leaving the four of us alone. As the door was closed, Kai clapped his hands together in an exaggerated manner.

"Now that I have most of the cast here, let's begin. Shall we?"

"Why have you summoned us both here?" Woodrow asked.

"Did you find out who killed my father?" Nikola added.

"Not exactly. There are a few things I'm still stuck on. I was hoping that you two could point me in the right direction." Kai gestured at the two individuals.

What is this? I thought as Kai continued. The confident attitude on display before was almost completely gone now.

"If there is anything you need, feel free to ask. I am at your complete disposal," Woodrow said.

"I appreciate the offer, but right now I need Nikola." Kai

useless, empty words. My gosh, people always want to throw sympathy upon those they deem as less fortunate. Hell, I often hear many of our staff refer to how oppressive my father can be. Yes, that's right, I'm fully aware of the rumors that are circling around about me. BUT SO WHAT?!" Nikola exclaimed.

Woodrow and I flinched, but Kai was unperturbed. Nikola continued, "Do you know what I hate the most about those kinds of people? It's that despite the many rumors and my father's oppressive way of doing things, not a single soul lifted a finger to help. They all turned a blind eye and pretended it wasn't happening. Or maybe they were just afraid of what daddy dearest would do in retaliation."

The gears in Kai's head turned rapidly as he digested all of Nikola's words. Her sadness had disappeared now. Her tears had dried and her face contorted with disgust and rage.

"However, you are correct, detective. I do indeed hate the man you know as Alderheim Evergreen, my father. The number of things I had to go through as the heiress of this family… Having to smile on command, having to be the perfect doll that could do no wrong. Despite trying to please my father and maintain our family image, nothing ever satisfied him. He made threats to cut me out of his will every time I misbehaved or didn't do something to his liking. Do you have any idea what that kind of hell is like?"

Woodrow cast sad, sympathetic eyes towards Nikola. Even Kai couldn't help but show a tinge of melancholy.

"Honestly, I don't understand what my mother saw in that man. She must've been so blinded by love that she didn't see what he truly was until it was too late."

"Maybe she was a gold digger," Kai interjected.

Nikola's eyes twitched. Woodrow was stunned by the

comment.

"I mean, your mother was very popular before she settled down. At the height of her career, she must have had her share of suitors. She probably picked Mr. Evergreen because he had the deepest pockets. She probably just wanted to retire in luxury." Kai shrugged.

What is he saying? I thought as I watched on. *It doesn't make any sense. Based on what the butler elf told us, Maria Swan was happiest while performing. She wouldn't have given it up for anything, let alone money. It was unfortunate that her parents fell on hard times that she had to do one grand show in order to alleviate their financial burden. The rest of the story ended in a typical fairytale romance. Kai knows this wasn't a case of gold-digging.*

"To be honest, it would make a lot of sense if your mother was only after his money. Plus, now her daughter stands to gain from the estate with Alderheim out of the way. Like mother like daughter, both were using this man for their own ends. Tsk, tsk," Kai said flippantly.

"I am nothing like my mother!" Nikola said fiercely.

"You and I both know that's not true. You are more like your mother than you give yourself credit for."

Enraged, Woodrow broke his silence. "Now listen here, I will not tolerate such blatant disrespect toward the late mistress. Did you call us here just to speak ill of the dead? Mr. Evergreen may not have been the best husband or father, but he did love his family."

"Funny you say that. Wasn't it you who told me that Maria died from the stress applied to her by Mr. Evergreen? And what about poor Maria, huh? I'll admit, Mr. Evergreen must've had a fondness for the aspiring starlet. All those rumors that surrounded her, it's a bit like what's happening to Nikola now," Kai explained.

Nikola was clenching her fist as Kai continued. When this was over, I was going to have to reprimand Kai for going too far.

"Those rumors are baseless and without merit. They only serve to destroy a person's reputation!" Woodrow cried out.

There was a glint in Kai's eyes now, as if he had been waiting for this moment.

"What makes you seem so sure about that?" Kai asked.

Taken aback by the question, the elven butler stammered a bit. "E-explain what? You know how people love to spread gossip and bring people above them down. It's all rooted in jealousy if you ask me."

"Interesting that you are so sure about Maria's innocence. Even when you were telling me her story, it seemed like you felt sorry for her. If you ask me, you almost seemed guilty," Kai pressed.

The color in Woodrow's face had drained while Kai spoke. Nikola looked confused as she witnessed the back-and-forth between the two. I was starting to understand what Kai was getting at.

From the beginning, the story had too much of a fairytale ending with a tragic epilogue. Is Kai trying to link a proper motive? If we say Nikola is our primary suspect, what would be her motive? Hating her father for being overly strict isn't enough, but revenge is. It seems Kai wants to pressure the butler into revealing the plot. Wait, that doesn't make sense. Why pressure him and not Nikola? Unless...

Admittedly, I struggled to see Kai's train of thought. In the end, I stared back and forth between them in anticipation.

"Don't be ridiculous. What do I have to be guilty about?" Woodrow asked.

Kai's demeanor turned serious as he stared at Woodrow.

"Does she know?" Kai asked coldly.

Nikola knitted her eyebrow as she stared at Woodrow.

"Do I know what?" she asked.

Kai returned to his usual self as he gave her a whimsical smile.

"How your parents really got together," Kai answered.

"How my parents really got together?" Nikola said, confused.

Woodrow's face blanched.

"What are you saying?" Nikola asked. "What does that have to do with anything?"

"Nothing at first, but if we really analyze the truth behind that union, it may give us more insight," Kai said.

"Insight into what?" Nikola asked.

"Why Mr. Evergreen is dead, of course."

"This is nonsense," Woodrow erupted. "How can a past marriage shed light on Mr. Evergreen's murder? Come, Miss Nikola, this is pure hogwash. We might as well wait for the proper authorities to handle this."

Woodrow reached a hand to escort Nikola out of the room. However, he was met with resistance as Nikola slapped his hand away.

"I'm curious," Nikola said.

"Excuse me?" Woodrow was dumbfounded.

"I'm curious about what the detective has to say. There should be no harm in hearing him out. If this is a tall tale, then we will simply dismiss his claims."

With the butler feeling deflated, he had no choice but to

acquiesce to Nikola's demand.

"Very well Miss. Well, you heard the lady, explain yourself."

Chapter XI

After receiving the green light, Kai stretched his arms overhead. After a brief moment of confused stares, he began.

"Okay, so let's start from the beginning. It's no secret that Maria Swan was a famous actress and dancer. So it would make sense for a woman of her caliber to acquire a lot of admirers, correct?"

"So?" Nikola answered.

"Your point being?" Woodrow asked.

"My point is that she has been eye candy for many men out there, especially those in power. It should come as no surprise that Maria received many advances from hundreds of men from different walks of life. Some rich and influential, others not, but can we pinpoint the main thing these guys have in common?"

"They all were die-hard fans of hers," I said, breaking my silence.

"Very good, Zed. Yes, they all were die-hard fans who would compete for her attention and always make it a point to see her shows before anyone else."

"You're just stating the obvious. Of course people would flock to see their favorite actor or actress in a show," Nikola said casually.

"Then it should be just as obvious that Alderheim Evergreen was among these die-hard fans." Kai revealed the black book from his shirt pocket.

"What the, how did you get that?" Woodrow bellowed after recognizing what was in Kai's hands.

Kai waved the book with a smile. Woodrow stared on in surprise.

"Oh, I see you recognize this. Well, to summarize for the lady, this is Mr. Evergreen's ledger. I happened to come across it during my investigation." Kai flipped through the pages of the book as he continued, "Mr. Evergreen was a thorough investor and kept track of all his money and the many business dealings that he was involved in. Which makes this transaction all the odder."

Kai pointed to a single entry at the end of the page.

Maria Swan, 5pm-7:30pm

"So what? He went to see my mother's show. Based on what you said, that shouldn't be strange at all," Nikola shot back.

Without saying a word, Kai turned to the next page of the ledger, which revealed a series of designated times and locations both in and out of the country. All those locations had roughly two or two and a half hours between them. These were clearly showtimes for a regular play. This left only one conclusion.

"Congrats, you've proven that Mr. Evergreen was a die-hard fan," Woodrow said curtly.

"Oh, he was so much more than that," Kai said.

"He was a stalker," I said.

"Precisely. A stalker with a serious crush. This book clearly shows that he consistently went to see Maria perform at every chance he could get. I suppose being rich gives you plenty of chances. However, it was not possible for Mr. Evergreen to get up and leave without anyone knowing his whereabouts. Sure, he might've lived alone, but he still had employees that worked for him, especially his servants."

Mr. Woodrow grew nervous at Kai's revelation. Noticing his reaction, Kai pressed the butler.

"You were aware of these trips weren't you, Mr. Woodrow?"

"But how can you be so sure?" Nikola asked.

"Because he was the only one we interviewed that had intimate knowledge about your parents. The maids were hired long after Maria's passing and they were just recently exposed to the various rumors. Henry Woodrow is the only one with a long enough tenure to speak about what happened back then. Am I correct, Kai?" I explained.

I was able to follow Kai's reasoning to some extent. However, I was still lost as to how this all leads back to Mr. Evergreen being murdered.

"Nice job, Zed" Kai said as he tossed a treat towards me.

Woodrow took out a handkerchief to wipe his forehead as sweat trickled down.

"It's true," Woodrow said.

A shocked Nikola turned towards Woodrow.

"Wait, if he stalked my mother, wouldn't she have noticed the frequent meetings?" Nikola asked.

"That's the beauty of this. The book shows that he went to at least ten of Maria's performances. However, according to Woodrow's story, Maria and Alderheim met during one of her private shows. As for why she may not have noticed, I highly doubt Miss Swan was able to recall the faces of all the people that watched her show. She had plenty of fans and it would have been easy for Alderheim to keep his distance and avoid suspicion. But don't take my word for it, let's ask the butler himself," said Kai.

"Correct." Woodrow said.

The butler rubbed his temples together and let out a sigh. After taking a moment to collect himself, Woodrow continued, "When Master Evergreen was getting ready for one of Miss Swan's private shows, he made it a point that everything be perfect. He had confessed his plan to me, and said that he'd win her over by showing off his money and status. Although, as you heard in my story, such attempts proved to be fruitless."

"About that," Kai said. "There's something I find strange. Miss Swan initially rejected Mr. Evergreen's marriage proposal even after he'd made his best first impression. What exactly changed? Why did she end up marrying him?"

I ruminated on Kai's question. *Miss Swan and her family had fallen on hard times and Mr. Evergreen was able to bail them out. Kai and I both sat through that story. He should know. . . Wait a minute!*

"What's so strange? It's not hard to believe that my father helped my mother out financially. Most guys love to swoop in and be the hero for a damsel in distress. In return, my mother probably felt very grateful to him," Nikola explained.

"No," I interrupted. "Kai, stop jerking us around. You know exactly what was so strange." Nikola and Woodrow exchanged a glance between us. Kai gave a whimsical smile.

"Whatever do you mean?" he said, shrugging his shoulders. *I knew it.*

Kai was just playing around with us. He clearly knew the answer but liked holding us in suspense. A moment later, Kai raised his hands in mock surrender.

"Fine, fine. To answer Nikola, what is really strange was the coincidence of the whole matter," Kai said, while everyone listened intently.

"So it was coincidental that Maria's family was in financial trouble when Alderheim showed up, yes? Then after helping her, he and Maria decided to get married like it was some fairytale? I highly doubt that. There must be more to that story."

While Nikola and Woodrow were distracted listening to Kai, I slowly crept toward them with my teeth bared.

"The key to finding the truth is you!" I snarled.

I inched toward Woodrow and the cowardly butler backed away.

"I knew that Mr. Evergreen had a fondness for Miss Swan. However, I had nothing to do with whatever scandal went on between them. And as far as her financial troubles, perhaps she saw an opportunity to have an early retirement by marrying into the Evergreen family?" Woodrow pleaded as I inched closer.

"Even if I believed that, there are several holes in your story that debunk your theory," Kai said nonchalantly.

"Not that it matters. You've been lying almost this entire time," I added.

Woodrow backed himself against a wall with nowhere to go.

"Me, lying? I admit that I wasn't exactly forthcoming about Mr. Evergreen's supposed stalking, but I hardly see how that implicates me."

"Would you like to know how I know you're guilty?" I leaned in and whispered into the butler's ears.

"It's because I can smell your fear." Woodrow's eyes widened.

"You've been noticeably more concerned and frightened ever since Kai mentioned Nikola's mother in this case. As your fear has grown, you've been trying to dissuade us with other theories. Now, tell me why you would be so afraid unless there was a lot more that you're not telling us?" I asked.

Cold sweat appeared on Woodrow's face. The stench of his fear grew, confirming my suspicions. Determined not to give in, Woodrow fixed his tie and looked at Kai.

"Jeez, Mr. Kai, you mind putting your mutt on a leash?" Woodrow said.

"WHAT!?" I shouted.

"Oh no…"

That was the last thing I heard Kai say before my vision blurred into a glistening gold. My hind legs bent back further and I felt my clothes starting to stretch. My front legs and torso increased in size and I felt my thumbs stick out of my paws. My claws grew sharper, ripping up the carpet. Muscles expanded as the fur on my body rapidly sprouted, bristling to complement my added mass. While transforming, the only thing in my mind were flashes of a white room. My mouth dried up and the smell of acetone filled my nose. Images of a forest filled my mind, along with scenes of test tubes and fire. Soon, fire swirled around and spread everywhere. A painful memory I will never forget.

The bone structure of my hindlegs changed slightly and I rose onto them as I howled into the air. Now a Beast, I snarled down at Woodrow. His jaw fell open as he stared into my eyes. The butler's fear was so palpable that I could taste it. A grotesque excitement flowed through me as I bared my teeth. My claws pierced the wall behind him, inches away from his face.

"Who are we putting a leash on now?" I growled.

From such a close distance, I could hear his heart beating in his chest. The poor man looked ready to wet himself when my drool landed on his face.

"As you can see," Kai said, "I'm not sure how much longer I can control my friend. Unless you want to be his new chew toy, I suggest you stop messing around and tell us what we want to know."

"Is it true, Henry?" Nikola spoke up. "Do you really know more about what happened to my parents?"

There was a moment of silence as Nikola locked eyes with Woodrow, trying to find the answer written on his face. My impatience grew as I inched closer to Woodrow, making sure he could feel the heat from my breath on his face.

"I'm gonna need an answer soon, Jeeves," Kai said.

"For heaven's sake, fine! Now please call off your mongrel," Woodrow begged.

I snapped, but before I could rip out the elf's neck and feast on his heart, I heard a snap. Suddenly, I found myself right next to Kai, who had placed a hand on my head in an attempt to calm me down.

Confused, Woodrow opened his eyes and attempted to compose himself. The stench of fear still radiated off of him, causing my stomach to growl and my blood to boil. Kai produced a treat and tossed it into my mouth. After eating it, I shrank down back to my usual hound form. From the looks on their faces, Neither Nikola nor Woodrow knew what to make of the situation in front of them.

"But how?" Nikola asked.

"I suppose this means we have a deal, right?" Kai said to Woodrow, ignoring Nikola's question.

"I suppose we do," Woodrow said begrudgingly.

"I hope I don't have to mention that if at any time I believe you are lying…" Kai snapped his fingers and I growled for effect. With a sudden jolt, the butler quickly complied.

"I understand," he said. "What do you want to know?"

"For now, I just want you to confirm whether or not my theory is correct," Kai said.

Just as I thought, Kai already understands what happened, he just needed a reliable way to confirm it. As I waited in anticipation, I couldn't help but notice Nikola seemed disinterested in the conversation. I found her disposition slightly odd, especially considering what was going on.

"Mr. Evergreen decided to instigate the marriage, didn't he?" Kai asked.

Woodrow narrowed his eyes as if he could tell what Kai was getting at.

"What exactly do you mean?" Nikola asked. "Of course, my father instigated the marriage; he was the one that proposed."

Kai shook his finger at the comment.

"Evergreen stalked Maria constantly, admiring her from afar. And when he finally gave his proposal, he accepted rejection just like that?" Kai shook his head and then continued. "Plus, the idea that Mr. Evergreen was able to conveniently bail out the Swan family from financial troubles that happened at such a convenient time. No, I don't think so."

"From the way you're carrying on, I'd say you already know what happened," said Woodrow.

"Maria Swan didn't feel indebted to Alderheim Evergreen for saving her family from financial problems. Quite the opposite. He manipulated and blackmailed Maria into becoming his wife. When you rethink the order of events, this idea makes the most sense. Wouldn't you say so, Mr. Woodrow?" Kai declared.

"What do you mean 'rethink the order of events'?" Nikola asked.

Kai turned toward Nikola and sighed before explaining. "Consider this: why would Mr. Evergreen bother to keep track of all your mother's shows? Because he was a fan? Maybe a stalker with a crush? It was more than that. He was obsessed with Maria. So obsessed that he still had a giant picture of her in his private room connected to the trophy room."

"It wasn't just a picture, it was a kind of shrine dedicated to her," I said.

"No," Kai corrected. "Not a shrine, a trophy. It was no accident that the private room was secretly connected to his trophy room. Lastly, it's no secret that Mr. Evergreen was strict and controlling, correct?"

"Yes. Why?" Nikola answered reluctantly.

"Answer this question: someone with a lot of money and influence becomes obsessed with a popular icon but is rejected, how would such a person respond to that?"

The room fell silent. Feeling that this was my cue, I deepened my voice and began to speak.

"If I can't have her nobody will! If her love of the arts is what's in the way, then I'll just get rid of it so she can be all mine!" I felt my cheeks redden slightly at my performance.

"Exactly!" Kai exclaimed. "Don't you find it odd that those rumors came up after Evergreen was rejected? But don't take my word for it, let's ask Jeeves if I am correct."

Woodrow chuckled to himself as he listened.

"I didn't think you actually found the trophy room. In any case, you are correct. Master Evergreen did start those derogatory rumors and promptly blackmailed her into marriage. You were right to call him controlling and manipulative. The master wanted everyone to bend to his will, which made him a shrewd investor when dealing with competitors. When Master Evergreen was rejected, he was enraged. The possibility of being rejected was not something he'd considered. Maria was a strong-willed woman who was determined to not be shackled by anyone. The blackmail wasn't just to destroy her career. The master wanted to create a problem that only he could fix in order to become her savior. However, as the rumors began to spread, they did little to deter Maria from her passion. Confident in her truth, she just ignored what people said about her. It was admirable, her strength only made him want Maria more. So, the master decided to take on a more hands-on approach," Woodrow explained.

"That's what I'm curious about. How did Evergreen blackmail Maria?" I asked.

"It wasn't just Maria he blackmailed. It was the whole Swan family," Kai assessed.

Woodrow glanced at the two of us and shook his head solemnly.

"To think you learned so much in a short amount of time… You're correct. Master Evergreen decided to use the rumors as a way to offer his financial assistance. At first, the setup for Maria's comeback show was going swimmingly. However, this wasn't a charitable gift but a loan to keep the family indebted to him. After being shot down repeatedly by Maria while aiding in her comeback, Master Evergreen managed to buy the Swan Theater from the banks and threatened to foreclose on the property unless they agreed to his demands," Woodrow finished.

"In other words, the Swan family was held financially hostage. Maria's choice was to either marry the megalomaniac or have her family live in poverty," I said.

Woodrow nodded. Interestingly, Kai nodded in understanding.

"You're telling me that Evergreen managed to financially cripple the Swan family and seize their assets? But how did he get access to the Swan estate?" Kai asked.

"I'm afraid that's something even I don't know," Woodrow responded.

"Interesting," mused Kai. "So, my dear Nikola, it appears we have come full circle back to you," Kai said flippantly.

"Now look here, sir," Woodrow interjected, "I've answered all of your questions and told you everything that I knew. Yet you still accuse the lady of the house?"

"I must admit, the history lesson about the Swan and Evergreen union helped me to understand a few things. But that's all it was, I'm afraid," Kai said.

"With her motive being what, her mother? You heard my testimony. Nikola had no idea about the truth of her parents' marriage," Woodrow protested.

"It doesn't matter, Henry. Even if I had no idea how my mother was tricked into marrying that man, that doesn't change the fact that I was aware of the abuse going on during the marriage, not to mention the emotional abuse I suffered after my mother's passing," Nikola said weakly.

Kai paused, placing a hand on his chin. After a moment, he asked, "Did you kill your father?"

"No," Nikola answered.

Arching an eyebrow, Kai continued to press.

"Then did you know Alderheim was going to die?"

"How would she possibly know that?" Woodrow protested.

"After Alderheim's speech in the ballroom, he went to his study. Around that time, Nikola had also seemingly disappeared from sight, presumably to follow him. She was the first one at the scene of the crime. What's more, you even had knowledge and access to a spare key," Kai said.

"So what? I live here. It shouldn't be strange that I know where the spare key is. Woodrow and the other maids know where the keys are as well in case of an emergency," Nikola answered.

"If you're referring to Elizabeth and Mary, they didn't know anything about a spare key. Care to explain that?" Kai said.

"Those two were recent hires, they haven't even been with us for long. I must've forgotten to relay that information," Woodrow explained.

"You conveniently forgot to mention the important piece of information to your new employees?"

"Master Evergreen wasn't keen on making that public knowledge anyway," Woodrow said.

Kai arched an eyebrow.

"Then why did you go looking for your father?" Kai asked.

Nikola frowned.

"I was concerned. I told you my father seemed to have left the ballroom in a hurry. I wanted to see if he was alright and thought he might be in this study. When I arrived at his study, the door was locked."

"Why were you so concerned?" I asked.

"Because my father was acting strangely throughout the day."

"Since this morning?" Kai asked.

Nikola nodded her head and continued, "My father was

never for or against the holiday season. If anything, he saw the holidays as a chance to increase his investments when people shopped for their loved ones. But this morning he seemed to be actively annoyed."

Turning to Woodrow, Kai asked, "Why did Mr. Evergreen decide to host a Christmas party?"

"It did seem spur of the moment. Usually the master made time to go to holiday parties to keep in touch with business connections and the like. I figured he had grown tired of that and wanted to invite them all at once, saving him the trouble of multiple trips."

"Anything else strange?" Kai insisted.

"Well, it was nothing really. However, Mr. Evergreen insisted on taking care of the guest list personally."

A smirk slowly appeared on Kai's face. Something was starting to click in his head.

"Well, Kai? What have you learned?" I asked.

"There are a few details I'm stuck on, but I do know two things for a fact," Kai said.

We all listened intently.

"First, I believe that Mr. Evergreen knew his life was endangered."

"How did you come to that?" Woodrow asked in shock.

"If you think that's shocking, wait until you hear the second thing I've learned," Kai said nonchalantly.

Kai pointed his finger and said, "*You* are the cause of Mr. Evergreen's untimely death."

Chapter XII

Everyone stared with wide eyes. Kai had accused none other than Nikola with her father's murder. After a moment of silence, the surprise on Nikola's face subsided and a small chuckle escaped her mouth.

"Hah, is this supposed to be a joke?" Nikola asked.

"My sentiments exactly, this is the third time you have accused lady Nikola," Woodrow barked.

"I assure you both that I am very serious," Kai said.

"Then explain yourself. How did you come up with such an accusation!?" Woodrow demanded.

I clapped my hands as a way to ease the tension. No longer wanting to stand on all fours, I changed back to my human form.

"Relax, folks. Kai will get to your questions, but there is a proper order to these things." *Plus, he loves making a grand show.*

"So, how did you know Evergreen knew his life was in danger?" I asked.

"Thank you, Zed. And to answer your question, I'm basing my accusation on the fact that Mr. Evergreen's behavior changed after he received a certain letter in the mail. My guess is the letter was some kind of threat," Kai explained.

"You guess?" Woodrow protested.

"Actually, I don't have to guess. We can all have a look for ourselves," Kai said and then reached into his breast pocket and pulled out a familiar envelope and another piece of paper.

"Woodrow, the letter Mr. Evergreen received in the morning looks similar to the one I'm holding, correct?" Kai said.

"Yes, but you said that wasn't the same letter."

"It isn't, because this was the letter I received this morning. However, I believe Mr. Evergreen received the same message as I did."

Kai opened the envelope, revealing the letter inside to show.

"No doubt the letter was a threat of some kind that was delivered to Evergreen, which may have been the cause of his sudden strange behavior," Kai continued.

"How do you know for certain that the letter was a threat to my father?" Nikola interjected.

"I can't say for certain. However, if we consider the fact I had to yank this out of Evergreen's body."

Kai opened up the piece of paper he found inside Mr. Evergreen to reveal the words written.

"As you can see, the style and handwriting match the letter I received in the morning. I am ninety percent sure that Mr. Evergreen and I received the same message," Kai concluded.

Nikola looked more annoyed than usual, and I suspected that Kai noticed this too.

"How can you be so certain? And why did you also receive a letter?" Woodrow asked.

"Look at the words written on my letter. It said, 'Don't be a naughty boy, or you might get a stocking full of coal.' It was a warning to dissuade its intended reader from a particular course of action lest they be punished. Zed, if you would be so kind as to read the second letter."

"'Oh, dear child, did I not forewarn thee? Naughty boys are only worth their lump sum in coal.'" I read aloud.

"What do you make of that?" Kai asked.

"Based on the wording, it appears to be a response to the previous letter. As if saying, 'I warned you about what would happen,'" I answered.

"It is exactly as my companion explained. When I first read the letter, I thought the culprit was taunting me after I failed to prevent Mr. Evergreen's death. I've since had a different train of thought."

"Which is?" Nikola asked.

"Before that, allow me to answer Woodrow's second question. Why did I also receive a letter? It's quite simple, actually. If we follow my reasoning about what the first letter implied, then the second letter was trying to discourage my involvement in today's proceedings. In other words, they wanted me out of the way so they could carry out their murderous plot. What's the best way to get away with murder? Make sure the great detective is absent from the case," Kai laughed.

"But why you, specifically?" Woodrow pressed.

Dusting his hands, Kai explained as he paced around the room.

"Two very clear reasons. First, because the culprit finds my presence to be a nuisance to their plans. Secondly, they were aware that I was invited to the Christmas party. Think about it, I had never met Alderheim Evergreen before. Of course, he may have heard about me due to my profession. However, he and I weren't even acquaintances, let alone friends. That means the only connection Evergreen and I had was that he invited me to his party. As to why Evergreen invited me would be the same reason that culprit sent me the advanced warning. Mr. Evergreen knew his life was endanger and thought inviting a detective of my caliber would be sufficient protection to the coming threat."

"You firmly believe that the culprit belongs to the Evergreen household because of that?" Woodrow said, exasperated.

"What he's saying is he's sure that I'm the culprit," Nikola spoke firmly.

Kai stopped walking at Nikola's declaration. After a few seconds, Kai turned to Woodrow and asked, "Mr. Henry, you said that Mr. Evergreen tended to the guest list personally?"

"That is correct."

"Who was in charge of the invitations?"

"One of the maids were in charge of that, it was—"

"Elizabeth, I presume," Kai finished.

Nikola's face turned pale when Kai narrowed his eyes in her direction. Kai smirked as if he finally managed to corner his prey. Then he resumed pacing and launched into a monologue.

"You asked what I thought when I found that letter on Mr. Evergreen's body. If we believe that Evergreen knew he was endangered, he must've known the reason. He was a shrewd investor and he had managed to entrap your mother in a marriage for the sole purpose of possessing her. I suspect there was a long list of people hoping to get a shot at Evergreen. The people on the guest list are innocent, as they would have had to know that I was also on that list. That means only people living in the Evergreen manor could've known about the guest list."

Kai briefly paused as he adjusted his voice.

"Now, Ms. Nikola, to your question. We know that

whoever wrote those letters had a vendetta against Alderheim Evergreen and we just learned that Elizabeth was in charge of delivering the invites. Elizabeth was more of a recent hire. What stake would she have in all of this? Unless she befriended a certain someone of the house, someone that regularly confides in her. Someone that could quite easily peek at the guest list. This person would also have to have an intense hatred for Evergreen, and we know that Alderheim was very controlling. Whoever did this had endured that torture for years. What do you make of that, Ms. Nikola?" Kai explained with a smile for the young heiress.

Nikola was silent. Woodrow glanced between the two before intervening.

"What exactly are you getting at?" Woodrow asked.

Kai rolled his eyes as the annoying butler placed his body between Nikola and Kai.

"What I am saying, Mr. Woodrow, is that given all of the evidence, there is only one logical conclusion. Nikola had a hand in her father's demise," Kai said, pointing at the accused.

The silent tension in the air was palpable. Nikola and Kai stared each other down. In the face of these mounting accusations, Nikola did not look bothered or afraid. She was poised, meeting Kai's gaze head-on.

"Hah! Hahahahah! You must be joking. Do you really believe in such a ridiculous claim? I killed him? For what, because I found living with my father to be so unreasonable?" Nikola asked.

"Unreasonable?" Kai countered. "Is trying to write his daughter out of the will unreasonable?"

Nikola's laughter came to an abrupt halt. Her eyes narrowed on Kai.

"Elizabeth managed to fill me in on the behind the scenes. It must've been a pain to always follow your father's orders; he wanted you to be the perfect heiress, another one of his possessions to control. Unlike your mother, you weren't willing to be subservient to him. You wanted to go your own way. It wasn't that easy, was it? Alderheim Evergreen has proven to be a master at bending people to his will. After all, he succeeded in ensnaring your mother. So, what did he do? He threatened you with the only thing he could, your inheritance. It was simple, if you wanted to keep your inheritance you had to do what daddy dearest said."

"You expect us to believe such a ridiculous claim?" Nikola said, crossing her arms.

"Ridiculous, yes, but I intend to prove it," Kai said resolutely.

"Prove what? That I had nothing to do with my father's murder?" Nikola shot back.

With the tension between them growing, Woodrow and I dared not speak.

"If you truly had nothing to do with it, then explain to me who else could've had the motive and the opportunity? You were the only one that wasn't accounted for in the ballroom that had knowledge and access to the key to the victim's study," Kai accused.

"You act as if the only way in the study was with the key. What about the outside? The culprit could've gotten in through the window, killed my father, and then left the same way he came" Nikola countered.

"Not possible," Kai objected. "There's a howling blizzard outside. And if someone had gone through the window, the carpets would have been wet with melted snow that would've tracked in. As you can see, the carpet is still dry."

"How convenient that you have an explanation for everything yet you still can't prove anything," Nikola refuted.

"Then tell me, why did you really go to Mr. Evergreen's study?" Kai pressed.

"I already told you."

"No!" Kai said sharply. "I want the real reason. You're the only person with knowledge and access to that key. Do you really expect me to believe that you conveniently felt like checking on daddy dearest? If I were you, I'd start taking this situation seriously and start talking." Kai stared at Nikola and awaited her response.

Nikola bit her lip, frustrated.

"I did it."

The words echoed throughout the room. I looked around to see who had confessed.

"What?" I exclaimed.

"You heard me. I killed Master Evergreen." Woodrow confessed.

"Liar, you were in the ballroom at the time of the murder, just like everybody else," I countered.

"I knew all of the Master's meetings. I was also in charge of delivering his mail. I could've easily slipped in that threatening letter he received. As the head butler, I could've asked Elizabeth to show me the guest list," Woodrow explained.

"Hmph. I don't doubt that Elizabeth would be more than willing to corroborate that story. However, Mr. Woodrow, if you expect me to be convinced of your guilt, then explain to me how you managed to kill Evergreen while you were in a separate location," Kai said.

"Simple, Master Evergreen had told me in advance that he would retire into his study at some point during the party. He was adamant about not being disturbed at that time. However, he made sure to check with me that refreshments were sent to his study in preparation."

"What specifically did Alderheim request and why?" Kai interjected.

"Milk and cookies. As to why, I figured he wanted a treat to satisfy himself while away from the public view," Woodrow answered.

"How does that prove you killed Evergreen?" I asked.

"Because I added poison," Woodrow said resolutely.

I caught a brief smile on Kai's face as he listened to the butler's explanation.

"Mr. Woodrow, you've been in Evergreen's service for over a decade. If you expect me to really believe that 'the butler did it,' you'll need to explain your motive?" Kai asked.

"Woodrow…" Nikola said softly, almost pleading.

"It's quite alright, Miss." Woodrow attempted to comfort Nikola before returning to Kai. "I told you, Mr. Evergreen drove Maria to her death. He may not have killed her directly, but he took away what she valued most. A talent like hers was meant to soar through the sky. But because of that tyrant, her wings were clipped, and for what? To be paraded around like a trophy? To be controlled like a puppet on a string?"

"So, it was vengeance?" Kai interrupted.

"How would you feel, detective," Woodrow queried, "if you saw someone you loved slowly drained? Becoming nothing more than a husk of their former self."

"Woodrow, please," Nikola begged again.

Her plea fell on deaf ears as Woodrow continued.

"Yes, I killed Mr. Evergreen, but it wasn't just for revenge. I saw how strong Nikola tried to be day after day. She is the spitting image of her mother. But as the days went by, Evergreen's hooks sank deeper into her. Slowly but surely, she was suffering. I killed Mr. Evergreen to protect Nikola."

"Stop this, you don't need to do this," Nikola protested. Yet, she was still ignored.

"I couldn't just watch as what happened to your mother started happening to you. I swore to myself that I wouldn't." Woodrow was trying hard to squeeze out the words. "I was powerless then, but I am not now. So, arrest me. Nikola is innocent, I'm the one you want." Tears fell from Woodrow's eyes.

"You old fool, you didn't have to do this," Nikola said, holding back her tears.

"She's right, you are an old fool." Like a knife cutting through the melodrama, Kai interrupted the moment without an ounce of remorse.

"I beg your pardon?" Woodrow replied.

"I mean, it's not a bad story, but your confession is pure fiction. It was convincing save for one detail," Kai continued, unbothered.

"What are you talking about?" Woodrow asked.

"I'm referring to the fact that Evergreen didn't die of poison. And even if he did, I already concluded that the confections given to him had nothing poisonous in them for three reasons. One, I tested the drops of the leftover milk in the glass and, as you can see, I'm still alive," Kai said.

"That's because the poison was baked into the cookies," Woodrow protested. Ignoring this, Kai continued while pointing at me.

"The second reason is—"

"I would've been able to smell any traces of the poison. I

sniffed all around the scene and there wasn't any poison to be found. Not in the cookie crumbs nor on Mr. Evergreen's body," I explained.

Woodrow's face clammed up.

"Lastly, the third reason, Evergreen doesn't like sweets."

Kai's words echoed in the room for a moment.

"But you already knew that, Mr. Woodrow. Your mistake was not thinking I would figure it out, but she did," Kai gestured to Nikola.

"Wait, how'd you know Mr. Evergreen hated sweets?" Woodrow asked.

"Simple, Elizabeth told me your late boss always preferred to have his coffee black. Hard to imagine a person like that would all of a sudden develop a late-night sweet tooth. Am I correct, my dear?" Kai asked, now facing her.

"Yes," Nikola said reluctantly.

"Once again, we are left with only one conclusion. Nikola, would you care to explain yourself? You were the only one not accounted for at the time of the murder. You were the first one to arrive on the scene. You had knowledge, access to the spare key, and you had motive," Kai declared.

"All of that is circumstantial at best. Especially since you can't prove any of it," Nikola shot back.

"Then explain why you went to Evergreen when you did," Kai demanded but he was only greeted with silence as Nikola hung her head down.

"As I thought," Kai continued, "you can't answer because the only reason you would go to Evergreen's study was because you concocted a plan to kill him. You did it to secure your inheritance and to avenge your mother."

Silence filled the room again. No one tried to refute Kai's

words. Woodrow was on his knees, defeated. Nikola looked as if she'd resigned herself to this outcome. Even I found myself convinced by the result. Everything had seemed to fit. We had a killer and a motive.

Looks like this case is closed. I thought.

"Unless," I heard. "Unless this was all just a clever misdirection," Kai said with a wicked smile. Woodrow and I raised an eyebrow. Nikola's eyes widened. For the first moment since I got here, I could finally smell it. I smelled her fear. As the situation was evolving, I couldn't help but wonder, *what the hell was going on?*

Chapter XIII

Woodrow and I exchanged incredulous glances at Kai. A moment of silence passed. Kai was serious.

"What are you on about?" Woodrow shouted.

Truth be told, I was wondering the same thing myself.

"What I'm saying is there's a lot more to this story," Kai answered.

"What do you mean more? You've been pinning the blame on Nikola this entire time and now you're taking it back?" Woodrow asked.

"As much as I hate to admit it, he has a point, Kai. You said that Nikola was the only person with motive and access to Alderheim's study," I added.

"Correct. She was the only one we know about, but what if there was another culprit in the room?" Kai mentioned.

"You're talking in circles. You just made it clear that Nikola was the only one with access, not to mention that she was the only one unaccounted for during the time of the murder," Woodrow explained.

The smile on Kai's lips never faded.

"There's always been something I found strange about the timing. Why did Evergreen go to his office right after his speech?" Kai asked.

There was a hanging silence, one I didn't bother to fill because I knew Kai was sitting on the answer.

"I figured you would know the answer, Mr. Woodrow. But here's a hint."

Kai presented the butler with Mr. Evergreen's ledger, revealing a page with a date and time written down. *December 25*th*. 12 am.*

"Mr. Woodrow, weren't you the one who mentioned that Evergreen had made an appointment at 12 tonight? It's written down here."

"So?" Nikola said hesitantly.

Kai ignored her and continued talking with Woodrow. "You had no idea who Evergreen was trying to meet, right?"

"That's correct. He only informed me of the meeting time," Woodrow said.

"Interesting. So, no one knows exactly who Alderheim was waiting for in his study," Kai said.

"It could've been one of the many business partners my father had invited. A lot of people were looking to get into business with him," Nikola said.

"There are a few things wrong with that, my dear," Kai began to explain. "For starters, I ran through the entire guest list with Elizabeth. Thanks to her, I was able to conclude that everyone was accounted for in the ballroom, except for Nikola, of course."

"We know already, that's the main reason you were accusing her in the first place!" Woodrow exclaimed.

"Then who was the meeting with?" Kai asked.

"What does it matter?" Woodrow yelled.

"It matters a great deal actually," Kai continued. "Several guests were at this party, yet not one person made a move after the speech. Everyone stayed and joined in on the countdown."

"Except Nikola," I finished.

"Did Nikola set up a meeting with her father?" I asked.

"I thought the same way, but I had a few problems with that theory." Kai said as he held up three fingers and continued. "First, why didn't Nikola immediately go to Mr. Evergreen's study when he did? It wouldn't have seemed odd for a daughter to retire with her father. Answer, she was supposed to stay in the ballroom to keep me entertained.

Nikola stared daggers into Kai, but her fear was still present.

"Don't look so angry. From the moment I met Mr. Evergreen, I noticed how he firmly told you to be on your best behavior. I bet daddy dearest wanted to make sure I was preoccupied," Kai answered.

"That would explain her strange behavior during the countdown," I added.

"Exactly. Now to my second point, why was the door locked? Only people who live in the manor would be aware of a spare key. Everyone in the ballroom, including the butler and maids, were accounted for except Nikola. In addition, if we believe that Nikola found the door to the office locked, what does that mean?"

Kai was grinning from ear to ear. His riddles were getting annoying, but the more I thought about it, the more I was starting to understand.

"Wait a minute," I continued, "if we take what Kai said as fact, then that means Nikola might not have been the last person to see Mr. Evergreen alive. And if that is true, then the idea of Nikola being our main suspect is almost completely destroyed."

"Now you're starting to get it," Kai said.

As I was pondering the evidence, an unmistakably strong scent filled my nose. I found myself drooling, it was intoxicating. It was the smell of fear seeping out of Nikola. Once I realized who it came from, I shook my head trying to regain my senses. I couldn't make sense of it.

We just discovered a new line of thinking that could get her off the hook. Why is she afraid?

"In other words," Kai continued, snapping me out of my thoughts, "the door was locked because the person Evergreen was waiting for had already arrived, the lock was to prevent them from being disturbed."

"I don't understand," Woodrow interrupted. "If you figured all of that out, why were you so insistent on pinning the blame on Nikola?"

In response to Woodrow's question, Kai said, "Where did the person that killed Evergreen escape to and what was their meeting about?"

"Escape?" Woodrow questioned.

"Ah, but before that," Kai said, facing Nikola, "my dear, you stated that when you opened the door, you saw Alderheim's body and nothing else, correct?"

Nikola hesitated as concern flickered across her face.

"Yes," Nikola answered.

"I see. Since Nikola is still sticking to her story, that means our potential suspect found a way to escape detection. And even if Nikola is lying, the culprit couldn't have left through the front door without being spotted by Zed and I. So, any ideas of where they went?" Kai asked.

"Don't tell me you're suggesting the culprit was hiding in this room the entire time." Woodrow said.

"Unlikely," I explained. "Between my nose and Kai's eyes,

we searched this room from top to bottom. Nobody is hiding here without us knowing."

"Where else could he have gone?" Nikola asked.

"The answer is simple. Outside," Kai said as a matter of fact.

A small chuckle escaped from Nikola.

"And here I thought you were onto something," Nikola said.

"I'm confused, what are you talking about?" Kai asked.

"Confused? You said it yourself that coming from outside was not possible. If the window was open, then the floor would be wet due to the blizzard blowing inside. It only stands to reason that escaping through the window would also be impossible," Nikola mocked.

"You're right, it wouldn't be possible to leave through the window. However, what if there was another way?" Kai asked. Nikola's brow knitted in consternation.

"What other way?" Woodrow said. "You said the person didn't hide, exit through the door, and climb out the window. What other way could they have gone? Are they a phantom or something?"

"No!" Kai exclaimed. "Those milk and cookies didn't eat themselves. We already know that Mr. Evergreen didn't eat them. Whoever was in this room was definitely a corporeal being."

All three options were shot down. What's left? We searched this room from top to bottom, and there are only two ways to get outside.

My thoughts were racing trying to figure out the answer. Then it occurred to me that the answer had to be in plain sight. I glanced at Kai, then looked around the room, trying to retrace our steps. I looked towards Evergreen's desk then turned my attention to the potted plant where we found the key. My eyes finally settled on what I was looking for. I knitted my eyebrows, then I took another look at Kai. Except this time, when our eyes met, I was greeted with a knowing smile.

"You can't be serious," I blurted out.

"Oh, but I am," Kai declared.

Nikola and Woodrow looked at us curiously.

"Care to share your answer with the class, Zed?" Kai asked.

"The fireplace," I answered reluctantly.

With a snap of his fingers, Kai responded, "That's right, the fireplace is the only other way someone could escape the room."

Nobody else was convinced by his declaration.

"Complete nonsense. How the hell could someone pull that off, and how are you so sure?" Woodrow questioned.

"How could someone do it? I admit I am still working on that." Kai continued. "As for how I'm so sure? Simple, after I investigated Evergreen's body, I turned my direction to the fireplace. After checking it with my hand, I knew the fire was only recently put out, as it still felt hot to the touch. But I couldn't make sense of it. I thought that maybe the window had been opened, allowing the excess wind to come in and blow out the fire. However, we have already disregarded that possibility. The other possibility was the fire extinguished due to a struggle between Evergreen and whoever he met with. Sadly, Mr. Evergreen's body didn't show any signs of defensive wounds or of being burned. With those most likely explanations debunked, the question still remains. Why was the fire put out? As a matter of fact, if the culprit were to leave the fire as was, it would have made their disappearing act more convincing. The explanation that makes the most sense was that the culprit needed to put the fire out in order to retreat up the chimney."

"Then you've lost," Woodrow said. "If we take your words as fact, that means the culprit is long gone."

"I wouldn't be so sure just yet," Kai said grimly.

"What do you mean?" Woodrow inquired.

"I mean, I don't think the culprit would leave without accomplishing their goal," Kai answered.

"Goal?" Nikola said.

"The place was ransacked. Someone was looking for something. The desk itself showed signs of forced entry. Not to mention all of the scattered papers," Kai explained.

"If that's the case, what was the culprit after?" I asked.

"It's no secret that Master Evergreen had enemies, but I doubt any of them would try to kill him. His investments benefitted other businesses," Woodrow answered.

"Actually, I was hoping to hear Nikola's thoughts on the matter," Kai said.

"Me? How should I know what they were after?" Nikola answered.

"Mr. Evergreen had a knack for blackmail. He blackmailed your mother into marriage. It wouldn't be a stretch to imagine that he would do it again. Only this time someone was willing to kill to protect their secrets," Kai answered.

"Then why ask Nikola that?" Woodrow asked.

Woodrow still continued to come to Nikola's defense when possible. By now, Kai had grown used to Woodrow's persistent loyalty.

"I'm still not convinced of her innocence," Kai shrugged.

"Unbelievable," Nikola said. "According to your reasoning, the odds of me killing my father are low, almost non-existent, yet you're still trying to blame me."

Tears were welling up in Nikola's eyes, but Kai paid no heed.

"You're right. Based on what we discovered, you should be perfectly safe from any murder accusations. However," Kai glanced at Nikola, "when did I ever say you murdered your father?"

Nikola's face froze and her eyes fluttered.

Kai flashed a grin as he said, "I said you had a hand in Mr. Evergreen's demise."

Nikola glared at Kai, but quickly relaxed.

"Look here," Woodrow objected, "your little mongrel over there can rip me to pieces if need be, but I will not allow any more slander of Nikola."

I growled, ready to make good on that promise. However, Kai raised a hand, signaling me to stand down. Annoyed, I held my place.

"Relax, Woodrow, he is just spouting baseless conjectures without a shred of proof," Nikola dismissed.

While I fought the urge to take Woodrow up on his offer to rip him to pieces, Kai still wore his unwavering smile.

"Are you sure about that?" Kai asked.

Nikola was silent, her eyes burning with determination.

"Zed and I searched through the desk. Sadly, we didn't find anything worth killing over. Although, I did find a bunch of these," Kai said, producing a few letters.

Woodrow stared at them, appearing confused. However, Nikola's eyes started to waver slightly.

"As I stated earlier, I had received a letter that warned me to stay away from today's proceedings. And we've learned that Mr. Evergreen also received a letter in the morning that inspired a meeting. We already know the letters were written by the same person. However, while investigating the desk, I was hoping to find the exact letter that put Mr. Evergreen in such a panic this morning," Kai explained.

"And was your search successful?" Nikola asked.

Kai shook his head.

"Unfortunately not," Kai said, much to Nikola's disbelief.

Kai was excited, like a magician getting ready to dazzle his audience. Although by that example, that would've made me the magician's assistant.

"But," Kai continued, "you can imagine my surprise when I found so many letters stuffed in that desk. Personally, I wondered why the culprit left all of them behind. Some had juicy information on ruthless deals that would make front page news."

"Is there a point?" Woodrow cut in.

"My point is that whatever the culprit was after was worth a lot more than all of this blackmail material," Kai explained.

"So?" Nikola asked.

"So, would you like to guess what these letters have in common with the one I received this morning?" Kai asked.

"They all came from the same person?" I offered. "If they all came from the same person, that would explain why Evergreen set up a meeting. Because he knew the person as a business associate," I concluded.

"That would make sense," Nikola chimed in. "It could've been an associate in charge of providing my father with information he could use in his deals."

"Way off," Kai interrupted. "It's not a bad theory except for the fact that the handwriting doesn't match," Kai said.

"Then what do the letters all have in common?" Woodrow asked.

"Absolutely nothing," Kai said, sporting a smile.

Silence fell as Kai began to laugh at our shocked faces.

"What the hell do you mean!?" Woodrow yelled.

Even I was irritated then, and I was about to grab Kai by the collar and shake him. Kai held up his hands in surrender before I could.

"I know, I was just as upset as you are," Kai continued. "I thought for certain the letters had a link between them. Turns out I was wrong."

Nikola eyed Kai curiously as he was feigning disappointment.

"Then why did you ask us about what the letters had in common?" Nikola asked.

Kai's smile returned as he said, "So nice of you to ask. The answer is simple. While the letters themselves have nothing in common, the envelopes they came in reveal so much. Specifically," Kai snapped his fingers as he showcased one of the envelopes, "these letters have the same address written on them. However, one of these envelopes is not like the others. Can you tell the difference?"

The silence was deafening. After his last stunt, not a single person dared to answer his question. Personally, I didn't want to answer either, as this game of whodunnit was getting annoying, but no one else was going to do it.

"The return address is different," I answered.

"Bingo. Although it would be more accurate to say the return address is switched. As you can see, with the letter Zed and I received, the address, Arctic Circle 37564, is written as the return address. But on this envelope, we see the same address as the recipient's and the return address is Evergreen Manor."

"So?" Woodrow interrupted. "All that would mean is Mr. Evergreen knew our suspected culprit and was in correspondence with them."

"This would also support the idea that the culprit is an old business partner of my father," Nikola added.

"Couple things wrong with that theory." Kai held out two fingers. "One, if Evergreen had contacted this person before, then why was the letter tucked away in his desk? Think about it. This letter was clearly supposed to be sent away. So why is it still in the Evergreen manor?"

"Perhaps Mr. Evergreen had second thoughts about sending the letters?" Woodrow answered.

"Then why not just destroy the letters if you had second thoughts?" I asked.

"More than that," Kai added, "if you look at this envelope, you'll see that it was cut open with a letter opener. Now tell me, if Mr. Evergreen intended to write and then send this letter, why would he cut open the envelope to read his own work?" Woodrow was speechless at the mounting questions. A cold sweat formed on Nikola's brow.

"What are you getting at?" she asked.

"This leads me to my second point," Kai continued, ignoring her. "It should be obvious that Evergreen didn't write this letter. I cross-referenced the handwriting from the letter I received with Mr. Evergreen's black book. Neither of them turned up a match. So that begs the question, who wrote it?" Kai paused, gazing at the letter. "After inspecting the letter, I learned that the writer is right-handed and that it was written with a feminine touch. And I'm sure Zed would agree that it has a hint of some expensive perfume. The writer is a right-handed woman with expensive taste."

Suddenly, all eyes were on Nikola.

"Nikola, you wrote this letter, didn't you?"

Chapter XIV

All eyes were on Nikola as we waited with bated breath. Kai pointed at the young heiress.

"Nikola, you wrote this letter, didn't you?" Kai asked.

"Wait," Woodrow interjected. "We don't know for a fact Nikola wrote that letter. The maids could've done it themselves."

"If one of the maids had done it, then Evergreen wouldn't have been able to intercept the letter. The maids would have mailed the letter themselves."

"But what about the perfume?" I added. "When I bumped into you guys at the countdown, she didn't have a scent on her, let alone perfume."

"That is actually a simple manner," Kai said. He was about to explain but was quickly cut off.

"Even if I wrote that letter, what does that prove?" Nikola asked.

"It proves that you know who our prime suspect is. And based on your brief correspondence, I'd say the two of you seem fairly close," Kai answered.

"If she knows, then this should be easy," I said as fur started to envelop my body and my claws started to grow. I was getting ready to extract information, but before I could, Woodrow stood in between Nikola and I.

"What is he planning to do?" Woodrow asked.

"I believe my partner is attempting to interrogate your mistress," Kai answered.

"Call him off." Woodrow demanded.

"Sorry, what? I can't hear you over the growling," Kai mocked.

"I said call him off!"

"I might be persuaded, if you answer one question for me," Kai said.

Kai grinned from ear to ear. "Does Nikola know who she was writing to?" Kai asked.

Both Nikola and Woodrow exchanged glances.

"Should I take that as a no?" Kai said.

"How should I know?" Woodrow stammered.

"What is he asking, Woodrow?" Nikola asked.

"When's your birthday?" Kai asked Nikola.

The question was completely out of left field. Nikola was unsure how to answer. My size was increasing and soon I was towering over them. Drool escaped my mouth as I readied myself to charge. The heiress and the butler exchanged concerned glances. After a moment of silence, Kai snapped his fingers, redirecting their attention back to him.

"Focus on answering my question, not my furry friend," Kai said.

Snapping out of her daze, Nikola finally answered.

"September 19th."

Kai's eyes lit up. "Stand down, Zed. I believe I have what I need to solve this whole mystery," Kai said with certainty.

"Are you serious?" Woodrow asked.

I knew better than to question Kai. One look of that glint in his eyes and I was convinced.

"Well don't leave us in suspense," I said, urging him on.

"Certainly, but before that, let's do a quick review of everything we learned so far," Kai said.

Kai closed his eyes and massaged his temple as he collected his thoughts. After a while, Kai took a deep breath. Then he began.

"This all started in the morning when Mr. Evergreen received some kind of threatening letter. We aren't privy to the details, but it was enough for him to take action. Evergreen probably sensed that his life was in danger. However, instead of calling the police, he decided to throw a holiday party instead. What better way for him to protect himself than with a house full of witnesses? This was a fatal decision. As he was making a guest list, he thought to invite me as well. Having a room full of witnesses was great, and a private detective would be invaluable. Unfortunately, someone—the culprit's accomplice— caught wind of this plan. Somehow, they got the guest list from one of the maids and learned of Mr. Evergreen's plan. Enter Zed and I.

"Around that same morning, we also received a threatening letter that warned us to stay away. I didn't think much of it at the time. I don't even like the holidays and was never interested in Evergreen's party, but a chance to foil a murderous plot? Count me in. Then the party began. Despite their lukewarm nature, Mr. Evergreen still greeted me personally. After a few pleasantries, he made Nikola keep an eye on me. Although, thinking back, his real intention was to keep Nikola out of reach. It's too bad he didn't realize this move kept me in check the whole night, which is exactly what the culprit wanted.

"After Evergreen's speech, he began to act strange, as if he was in a hurry. We learned that Evergreen was indeed hurrying to a meeting with an unknown person. I knew something was off, so I intended to tail Alderheim. Imagine my surprise when the culprit's accomplice stopped me. Of course, I didn't know that at the time. Perhaps if I did, I could've prevented this tragedy. Either way, I was brought back to the ballroom during the countdown. The accomplice did a good job keeping Zed and I confined in one place. Meanwhile, Evergreen was getting murdered and the accomplice escaped our notice. Phase two of this murder plot was slated to begin.

"After the murder was completed, the culprit rummaged through Evergreen's desk. During that time, the accomplice met up with the culprit. Giving enough time for the culprit to escape, the accomplice screamed. Zed and I quickly sprang into action. However, by the time we got there, the accomplice was placed in a prime position to mess with our perception of the case. Isn't that right, Nikola Evergreen, or should I call you the accomplice?"

There was a stunned silence that echoed throughout the room. The fear I smelled earlier had returned with a vengeance and it wasn't just from Nikola or Woodrow either.

"Any questions?" Kai asked.

"Did you come up with that theory yourself or did fido help you?" Nikola said derisively, prompting a growl from my throat. "Oh, shut up," she said. "Even if by some stretch of the imagination your nonsensical theory held true, it's just speculation. You can't prove any of it."

"We still have the letter proving you knew the culprit," I countered.

Nikola held up three fingers, then explained.

"All you've proved is that my controlling and obsessed father intercepted a letter that never reached its intended recipient. Even if you could prove I wrote it, which is a pretty big if, so what? All that shows is a coincidence of having the same address, but that alone doesn't prove it was for the same person. Lastly, if the letter itself was any confirmation of my guilt, the 'great detective' would've revealed as much."

Faced with this argument, I looked to Kai for some back up. He silently stroked his chin, looking neither bothered nor confident.

"Hmph. Just as I thought," Nikola said.

"How lovely," Kai finally said.

"What?" Nikola said, eyeing Kai suspiciously.

"I'm talking about you," Kai continued as a slight blush crept on Nikola's face. "Even now when I look in your eyes, I see the same fiery spirit your mother had."

"You dare bring Mistress Maria into this again?" Woodrow objected.

Nikola silenced him with a wave of her hand. The sudden red features on her face disappeared as she gave an icy glare at the detective.

"Why are you bringing up my mother again?" Nikola asked.

"Because it's true," Kai said as he revealed a broken picture frame. Inside was a picture of Maria and Alderheim. "You really are the spitting image of your mother. Determined, a sufficient actress, an accomplished dancer, and beautiful."

"What are you up to?" Nikola asked.

"Maybe he intends to flirt his way to a confession," I mumbled.

Kai tossed the old picture to me.

"Wouldn't you agree, Zed? Though it seems the only thing she got from her father was his ruthlessness," Kai said, smiling.

I had no idea what he was trying to tell me. I stared at the photo, but nothing immediately came to mind. I turned to look at Nikola then returned to look at the picture. I repeated this action a few more times until it suddenly stood out to me. I felt my eyes widen.

"Why didn't I notice this before?" I said.

"Because we weren't looking for it. Even I was embarrassed with myself, so don't beat yourself up," Kai reassured me.

The two of us both shared a hearty laugh at our predicament. On the other hand, Nikola's impatience was growing as Woodrow looked on with concern.

"What's so funny?" Nikola asked.

"What's funny is you," I said.

Before she could inquire further, Kai turned toward the elven butler.

"How much did you love Maria?" Kai asked.

Woodrow eyed Kai curiously.

"What are you talking about?" Woodrow asked.

"When you were talking about Maria, you were quick to blame your former employer for her demise. You seemed very sympathetic, mournful even. And you spoke about her with such sincerity," Kai said.

"What are you getting at?" Woodrow asked impatiently.

"I'm saying you two must've been pretty close."

"How dare you insinuate such a thing. To even suggest that I tried to lie with my Master's wife!" Woodrow protested.

"Relax, pointy ears. I'm not suggesting anything of the sort. What I wanted to ask is if Maria ever confided in you. Like what the argument between Maria and Alderheim was about years ago, the one that led to drinking herself to death." Kai said.

"You think I'd tell you? Even if I did, how does that help?" Woodrow objected.

"I already know the reason. I was wondering if Nikola knows," Kai said.

Woodrow's face went pale. Kai didn't seem like he was bluffing. Nikola was fuming.

"Stop pretending I'm not here. What don't I know? Tell me!" Nikola demanded.

"Have you ever wondered why Evergreen treated your mother so harshly after that argument? Why was he so enraged at the time?" Kai asked.

"You said it yourself; he was a megalomaniac. He saw my mother as a possession, not a person. Maybe he wanted to put her on a tighter leash," Nikola answered.

"How old were you when it happened?" Kai asked.

"I must've been barely five years old. So?" Nikola answered.

"Old enough for some of the differences to show," I remarked.

"Hey wait," Woodrow interrupted.

"You weren't old enough to remember the conversation," Kai said, ignoring Henry.

"Stop this," Woodrow pleaded.

"Stop what? What are you people getting at?" Nikola asked.

"What the butler has neglected to tell you," Kai started.

"I said stop!" Woodrow yelled.

"You are not the daughter of Alderhiem Evergreen," Kai revealed.

Silence enveloped the room. Nobody uttered a word. After what felt like an eternity had passed, snippets of laughter could be heard. Soon Nikola erupted in a fit of laughter.

"Really, is that what this is about?" Nikola said, trying to contain her amusement.

"You guys aren't serious, are you?"

The silence in the room spoke volumes. Nikola turned towards Woodrow but the butler found it hard to look her in the eyes. The reality of the situation slowly crept in as Nikola's face turned into shock.

"You knew? You knew and you never told me?" Nikola finally said.

"No. I- It wasn't like that. Master Evergreen forbade us from telling you," Woodrow said.

Kai had placed a hand on Woodrow's shoulder.

"I think you should explain everything from the beginning," Kai recommended.

Woodrow pulled away from Kai's hand and glared at him. If looks could kill, Woodrow would've had Kai explode right where he stood. Kai shrugged casually at the deadly gaze.

"How did you find out? This was one of our most guarded secrets," Woodrow protested.

"If that was one of your most guarded secrets, then it's only a matter of time before the Evergreen family is exposed," Kai mused.

"To be fair, this secret almost went completely over our heads," I corrected Kai.

"Fair enough," Kai shrugged.

"Answer me!" Woodrow demanded.

"It's simple, her eyes. I wasn't just flirting when I mentioned her eyes. Nikola has the same cool blue eyes as her mother," Kai answered.

"So?" Nikola said.

"The problem is that Mr. Evergreen had green eyes." I answered, showing the photo of Maria and Alderheim together. "Blue eyes are a recessive trait, so if one parent has green eyes the child will most likely have green eyes. Nikola's eyes are blue," I concluded.

"You said most likely, so it's not definite," Nikola objected.

"Normally yes," Kai answered. "However, what convinced me was when I visited Evergreen's trophy room. There were two portraits I found that were very revealing. The first one I found was of Maria. It looked like it was placed on a shrine, but everywhere else was a mess, as if someone had thrown a fit. It wasn't until I saw the second portrait that I was convinced Nikola wasn't his daughter. It was a picture of Nikola, except the eyes were crossed out with a brush stroke of green paint. This told me that not only were you not his daughter, but he knew about it, which would explain him confronting your mother," Kai explained.

Nikola looked speechless, and Woodrow gave a pained expression.

"Now that I have shown you ours, how about you show us yours?" Kai asked Woodrow.

Feeling there was no choice, Woodrow relaxed his shoulders. "Fine."

Interlude II

O*ver fifteen years ago...*
It was a simple day like any other.

"You must first shift your weight on your front leg, then find your balance in the Retire position. Then slowly use your body to turn and so finish in this position," the woman explained.

After the explanation, the woman performed a perfect pirouette.

"Okay, now you try, Nikki," the woman said.

"Alright Mama," a little girl said as she got into her stance.

"Wait," the mother interrupted, making small adjustments to the toddler's stance.

"Like this, Mama?" the little girl asked.

The mother nodded as the child pivoted and spun her body. While not as elegant as her mother, the girl managed two good spins. She only tripped when she stopped her spin, and then she stumbled backwards.

"Ow!" the girl yelped.

Tears welled up in the young girl's eyes until she heard the sounds of applause.

"Not bad for your first try, Nikki!" the mother praised.

"But I messed up, Mama."

"True, but it was a fine first attempt," the mother said as she picked up her daughter. "Remember this Nikki, life's a stage. We may fall, but what matters is how we get back up. And for a star, we accept nothing less than to get back up with style."

As the mother and daughter shared a warm embrace, the door to the room suddenly opened. An elf wearing a monocle made his way inside.

"Hi Henry!" Nikki said.

The young girl leapt from her mother's arms and ran to the butler. Used to the child's excitement, Henry kneeled down, ready to receive the child's hug.

"Good afternoon, Miss Nikola. You're growing more and more each day," Henry remarked.

"Afternoon, Henry," the mother said dryly.

"Afternoon, Mrs. Evergreen," Henry said.

The woman knitted her brow.

"How many times must I tell you? Call me Maria," she said curtly.

"Henry, Henry," Nikola called out. "Look what I can do," Nikki said as she quickly got into position.

Nikola twirled around in a pirouette, but this time, she managed to finish on both feet with only a little wobble. Maria smiled at her daughter's progress.

"Congratulations, Miss Nikola!" Henry said as he applauded. Maria gave Nikki a pat on the head.

"That's my little ballerina," Maria said.

"Mrs.- er, Maria," Henry interrupted, "Master Evergreen would like to have a word with you."

Maria flinched at the words.

"About what?" she asked.

"All I know is that it is an urgent matter," Henry said.

Before she could question further, "Mama, let's go see daddy so I can show him too." Nikola said.

Feeling helpless in the face of her little girl, Maria sighed and picked up Nikola.

"Let's go see what he wants," Maria said with Woodrow leading the way.

In the dining room, Alderheim Evergreen sat at the table with a newspaper in his hands. After a sip of tea, Evergreen looked at his pocket watch tentatively. Soon, Henry walked in.

"Master Evergreen, Lady Maria and Nikola are here to see you," Henry said.

When Maria walked in, Nikola jumped out of her mother's arms.

"Daddy, daddy, look at what I learned from Mama," the young girl said.

Mr. Evergreen had a stern look in his eyes as he watched the child. As Nikola was still getting into position, Evergreen waved his hand dismissively.

"Woodrow, I believe I specifically asked for just Maria, did I not?" Evergreen asked.

"Yes, sir," said Woodrow.

"Then explain to me why you felt the need to bring the child along as well?"

"Forgive me, sir. I had interrupted their Ballet lesson-"

"Ballet! Hmph," scoffed Evergreen. "Don't you have anything better to do?"

The young girl was taken aback by her father's gruffness.

"What's wrong with her wanting to learn?" Maria shot back.

Alderheim redirected his cold gaze to Maria's own fiery stare.

"Regardless," Evergreen finally said. "I have an urgent matter to discuss with Maria privately."

"Very well, sir. I'll look after Miss Nikola. Come along, miss," Henry said.

Woodrow held the young girl's hand as they took their leave. While Henry escorted the child, a forlorn look appeared on Nikola's face. She couldn't help but get one good look at her parents as the door closed.

"Henry, are daddy and mama going to fight again?" the child asked.

Henry was speechless. After a moment of contemplation, the butler knelt down and patted the child's head.

"Don't worry, Miss Nikola. They are just clearing up a misunderstanding. In the meantime, why don't you show me some of the other moves your mother has taught you?"

Nikola let out an excited cheer, and her face lit up with a bright smile.

Back in the dining room, the two adults sat across from each other in silence. Alderheim sipped his tea quietly, his eyes still on his newspaper. As silence kept passing between them, Maria was the first to speak.

"What was so pressing that you had to summon me and send our daughter away?"

Mr. Evergreen ignored Maria's question and took another sip.

"If you have nothing to discuss with me, I shall be taking my leave," Maria said as she proceeded to leave.

Before she was able to take two steps, he spoke.

"Your parents send their regards," Alderhiem said, still not looking up from his paper.

Maria froze.

"What's that supposed to mean?" Maria asked.

Evergreen finally lifted his eyes.

"It means your parents are enjoying a debt-free life thanks to me."

"You expect me to say thank you? Again."

"Do I expect you to show a little gratitude? Yes, that would be nice."

"Gratitude?" Maria guffawed. "Is this a joke? They were only in debt because of you!"

Alderheim raised an eyebrow.

"Nevertheless, you married me. As I recall, you practically begged."

"I was forced to."

"Come now, Maria. This was a marriage of convenience that benefited us both. No matter what nonsense you spout and can't prove. Even you must admit that deep down you've enjoyed yourself."

"Lies!" Maria denied.

"Oh, really? Who was it that begged me to stop the repo men from taking your family's theater?"

"That was before I knew the kind of person you are."

Alderheim abruptly rose out from his chair. Maria took a step back.

"Correction," Alderhiem snapped harshly. "That was before you realized you couldn't trick me like you did with your other suitors."

Maria's face flushed and she raised her hand to strike. Alderheim caught her by the wrist and stared fiercely at her.

"I do so much for you, and this is how you repay me?" Infuriated, Evergreen pushed Maria down. "Whose food has kept you well-fed? Whose warm bed have you been sleeping in? Who has lavished you in beautiful jewelry and trips around the world?" Evergreen shouted.

Sensing immediate danger, Maria tried to back away.

"Why, why are you doing this?" Maria asked.

"To remind you of something. That you belong to me!" Evergreen yelled. "I thought you would've realized after I dragged you off that stage. Despite all I've done to make you happy, you still felt the need to betray me."

"What are you talking about?" Maria asked.

"I'm talking about Nikola."

Maria's eyes narrowed.

"What, did you think I wouldn't notice?" Evergreen said.

"I don't know what you're talking about," Maria said.

"Ah yes, ever the actress. Cool under pressure. That's what I admire about you. But you and I both know the truth."

Though her fear rose, Maria's determined eyes never wavered.

"Those fierce eyes of yours," Alderheim continued. "They betray you even now."

Maria was confused until Alderhiem took out a piece of paper from his breast pocket. Her jaw clenched as she stared at the paper.

"You already know what this is don't you?" Evergreen said. "I was growing suspicious as to whether Nikola was really mine, so I decided to have a little test performed. I haven't looked at the results yet. I figured I'd give you a chance."

"A chance for what? To beg?" Maria scoffed.

"I want you to stop lying to me!" Evergreen shouted. "You've been deceiving me all this time, and after I've done so much. I'm giving you a chance to admit your sins or else..."

"Or else what?" Maria asked. "What can you possibly do to

me now? Divorce me? Ha! That would be a godsend. Then the whole world would know that 'the great' Alderheim Evergreen lost his famed trophy wife. What's next, beat me? Go ahead. I may not have proof of you putting my family through debt, but the moment you lay a hand on me I can go public. Someone will believe me, and your reputation would be forever stained. You already forced me to quit my career and nearly destroyed my reputation. There's nothing more you can take from me now."

Evergreen gave a wicked smile. That sadistic, domineering grin was able to send chills down Maria's spine.

"Come now, my dear, are you sure about that? Tell me, what's the best way to get to a mother?" Evergreen asked.

Maria's face froze.

"That's right. Through her children," Evergreen continued. "I don't have to lay a finger on you. And if Nikola turns out not to be mine, I'll have no reason to show her any special consideration. You may no longer care about your reputation, but if it comes out that Nikola is a bastard child, she will never know peace. Tabloids will circle her constantly. Do you really want that for her?"

"You wouldn't dare," Maria objected.

"Oh, but I would. Or have you not been paying attention?"

"What do you want?" Maria asked.

"Tell me the truth and all is forgiven. I'll even take Nikola in as my own. If you don't, well, I don't need to remind you that Woodrow is alone with your daughter right now."

Maria clenched her fist.

"Fine," she surrendered.

"That's a good girl. Now tell me everything," Alderheim coaxed.

Few minutes passed as Maria explained. Alderhiem seemed very pleased with himself all the while.

"Was that so hard my dear? Don't you feel liberated by the truth?"

Though Maria suppressed the urge to spit in the man's face, her sense of dread never waned. In a flash, Evergreen took off his belt and moved towards Maria. Alarmed, Maria took a defensive posture.

"What are you doing?" Maria asked.

"There is still the matter of you going behind my back and sullying yourself."

"But you said-"

"That was to forgive you for giving birth to Nikola and giving her safe passage in my care. However, the matter of your dalliance has yet to be dealt with."

Evergreen wore a malevolent smile as he approached Maria.

Desperately, Maria hollered, "If you do that, I'll scream. I'll tell the world. I'll-"

"Do nothing, not if you want to save your daughter from my wrath," Evergreen explained.

Tears brimmed in Maria's eyes. Each step Alderheim took made Maria's body tense.

"That's it, my dear, that's what I like to see. Now hold still," Evergreen said.

Elsewhere, a horrified look was on the elven butler's face as he listened in.

"Henry, you're not even paying attention," the young Nikola said.

Woodrow quickly snapped back to reality.

"Oh, sorry Miss, what were you showing me again?"

"Jeez, pay attention this time," Nikola said as she slowly got into position. "Mama told me this is called 'galloping.' It's very fun to do."

Nikola then proceeded to start galloping across the room. As she finished her demonstration, the young girl took a bow, and Henry showered her with a round of applause.

"Bravo! It seems your mother taught you well," Henry said.

"What's taking mama so long?" Nikola asked.

Suddenly, a loud slapping sound was heard reverberating through the halls of the manor.

"What was that?" the little one asked again.

While not as good an actor as Maria, Woodrow did his best to feign a bright smile.

"It's probably just a ghost haunting these very halls," Woodrow said in jest.

"Not funny, Henry," Nikola pouted.

"Don't stop now, show me what else you've learned."

Nikola wasted no time in taking up Henry's offer. However, Woodrow was still plagued with the noises he kept overhearing.

A few years later.

"Again," a voice rang out over the music playing in the background. A young girl quickly proceeded to put on an elegant performance around the studio. She moved with precision and glided across the studio.

"Get ready for the big finish!" a voice rang out.

On cue, the young girl leaped into the air. As she landed, the music was immediately cut.

"Stop, stop, stop! It's all wrong," the voice yelled out.

"What's wrong now, mama?" the young dancer asked.

"I've told you many times Nikola, a *grand jete* needs to be perfect. Your front and back legs need to be perfectly aligned, as if you're doing a leaping split in the air. When you do it, it looks like you're doing a half-split again!"

"Again? I've been practicing the same routine all day," Nikola complained.

"Yes, and you're going to keep doing it until you get it right," Maria said.

Suddenly there was a knock at the door. After the signal was given, the elven Butler walked in.

"What do you want, Woodrow?" Maria asked.

"Master Evergreen requests a word with you, Maria," the butler said.

Calling it a request was only a courtesy. They both knew better. Maria's shoulders dropped and her hands trembled slightly.

"Nikola, do some light stretches and that will be all for today," Maria ordered.

"But what about going over the routine again?" Nikola objected.

"Just do as you're told!" Maria snapped.

Taken aback by her mother's sudden outburst, Nikola looked down and turned away. Coming to her senses, Maria attempted to say something.

"It's best not to keep the master waiting," Henry explained. "Come now, I'll look after Nikola while you're away," Henry tried to reassure her.

Maria had no choice but to comply. As she took her leave, Maria took another look at her daughter. Nikola was trying her best to hide her frustration.

"Why the long face?" Henry asked the girl.

"I'm fine," Nikola said.

"Nikola, I heard what happened through the door."

"I said I'm fine," she protested.

"Are you sure?" Henry probed.

"Okay, fine. It's a little annoying sometimes how strict Mama is all the time. It's like nothing I ever do is good enough for her," Nikola said.

"You ought to remember that your mother didn't become so good at her craft by being a slouch," Henry said.

"But that's just it, we barely find time to practice and when we do, she becomes a complete slave driver until dad calls her. Then she just drops everything and leaves me to practice on my own. It's so frustrating," Nikola said.

Woodrow was at a loss for words before saying, "Look, I know it's hard to see now, but everything your mother does is for you. Your mother has not and will not stop caring for you," Woodrow said.

"Yeah, I know," Nikola said half-heartedly.

"You know what?" Henry continued. "Why don't you show me some of the other routines you've learned?"

A smile crept on Nikola's face. "Okay, but these might be a little hard for you to follow," Nikola said.

"I'll try to keep up," Woodrow said.

Chapter XV

We all stared on in horror after hearing the terrible tale. Everyone except for Kai, who looked neither horrified nor concerned. Instead, he was stroking his chin.

"And that's how it happened," Woodrow concluded.

"All this time…" Nikola said, her fist shaking. "All this time you knew?"

"Not directly. I overheard the conversation between them, through the walls," Woodrow explained.

"You can do that?" I asked.

"These ears of mine aren't just for show. Within the manor, there aren't many sounds that escape my notice," Woodrow explained.

"Who cares about that!" Nikola shouted. "You knew the truth about my mother. All this time I thought she hated me. I always wondered why she was so strict, why she became so miserable, and why she drank herself to death. It was all because of me."

Nikola tried hard to fight the tears, but it was no use.

"Your mother was trying to protect you," Woodrow proclaimed.

"What good is that when she's dead? She died and I was

stuck under that man's thumb. And you did nothing to help! You knew this whole time that Evergreen wasn't my real father and said nothing!" Nikola bellowed.

"It's true, I've known the truth for years now."

"More than that," Kai interrupted, "it was you that helped Evergreen with the paternity test."

Woodrow glared at the detective as Kai shrugged.

"How did you find that out?" Woodrow asked.

"It was common for you to spend time with Nikola while her parents are away. Not to mention the underlying threat Alderheim gave to Maria about you 'looking after her daughter.' If anyone was the first to notice Nikola's discrepancies, it most likely would have been you. This would also aid your guilty conscience, which is why you were so ready to fall on your sword for Nikola earlier," Kai answered.

"You don't miss a beat, huh?" Woodrow said.

Suddenly, a loud slap reverberated in the room. The atmosphere was tense as a teary-eyed Nikola struck the butler across the face. Woodrow was in a daze. Snapping out of his shock. Woodrow pleaded with her.

"It's true, but I was sworn to secrecy. Neither your mother nor Alderheim wanted you to know the truth of your origin. Your mother begged me, and Alderheim made sure to enforce it. I know it's no excuse, but since your mother left us, I had to honor her last wish." Woodrow bowed his head and kneeled on the floor. "Please forgive me. If I could go back-"

"You can't," Nikola interrupted.

"Something's bothering me," I said. "We solved *why* Evergreen was so possessive of Maria and by extension Nikola, and possibly *how* Evergreen was killed, but who actually killed the man?" I asked.

"You mean you haven't figured it out yet?" Kai asked.

Woodrow immediately sprang up from the ground.

"You know who did it?" Woodrow asked.

"Sort of," Kai said with a mixed expression.

"What do you mean?" I asked.

"I mean that, I have a vague idea, but proving it may be difficult," Kai mumbled.

Nikola wiped her tears. Kai was deep in thought and tapped his forehead while we looked on in anticipation. After a few seconds...

"Ahem. I, the Great Detective Kai shall reveal the culprit!" he yelled.

A few more seconds passed by as Kai clicked his tongue.

"Plan B it is," Kai continued. "Okay, so let's look at the facts of the case. Who had the most to gain from Evergreen's death?"

A collective sigh followed the question.

"Not this again," Woodrow said.

"That's right, Nikola is the only one here that really benefited from Alderheim's death," Kai declared.

"You're more persistent than some of my old suitors. I always disliked clingy guys," Nikola said.

Paying no heed to the provocation, Kai continued, "Think about it. Someone like Evergreen had wealth and assets. But what would happen if he suddenly died? Answer: It would go to his next of kin or heir. Which should've been Nikola."

"But if the truth ever came out Nikola wasn't his daughter, she wouldn't get a cent," I added.

"So what? If anything, that gives me more reasons to keep him alive," Nikola argued.

"Not necessarily," Kai rejected. "The only people that know the truth about Nikola are in this room. Not even your maids were privy to the truth."

"What does that prove?" I asked.

"Let's reexamine the crime scene once more," Kai said and moved toward the desk. "I previously mentioned how this place seemed as if it was ransacked. Specifically, Evergreen's desk. I incorrectly assumed the culprit couldn't find what he was looking for. Although, if we reverse our thinking and assume the culprit succeeded, what could they have been after?"

"They were possibly trying to erase all evidence of Nikola's actual parents," I answered.

"Exactly," Kai agreed. "Evergreen was a lot of things. Cruel, sadistic, possessive, maniacal, controlling, but he wasn't stupid. There's no way he'd let someone else's daughter inherit his fortune. Naturally, he left a paper trail behind that revealed Nikola's origin in case something happened. Evergreen probably held on to the paternity test as an insurance policy. But if you eliminate all of the evidence, then the whole Evergreen fortune would be hers for the taking."

"So now my motive was money with a side of revenge? How cliché," Nikola said.

"Maybe," Kai said. "But I'd venture there's a deeper reason."

Nikola arched an eyebrow at the declaration. The supposed heiress didn't look too concerned as she placed a hand on her cheek.

"You wanted to be free, didn't you?" Kai asked.

Nikola was silent at Kai's question, so he continued, "Evergreen had a habit of threatening your inheritance to keep you in line and well-behaved. But there was more than that, wasn't there?"

Nikola instinctively covered her wrists.

"He probably forced you to behave in a certain way, maybe even cozy up to some rival investors to help stay ahead of the competition. It's like he was gro-"

"Enough," Nikola interrupted. "Get to your point."

"My point," Kai continued, "is that at some point you learned that Evergreen's threat to your inheritance was an empty one. You were never going to get a single cent. You were the man's puppet, and you were trying to find a way to cut the strings. A plan was hatched: destroy the evidence of your origin and clear the path to inherit a fortune."

"That's nice and all, but how does the culprit's identity come into play?" I asked.

"I'll admit, that was a little tricky to figure out. But again, if we look at the case with this new set of information, it becomes obvious. As I explained before, Nikola was just the accomplice. The real culprit was the mastermind," Kai said.

"Could one of the maids have done it?" Woodrow asked.

"A hired hitman?" I added.

"Wrong on both counts," Kai corrected. "For starters, the maids didn't know Nikola's secret, plus they have an alibi during the time of the murder. A hired hitman would be impossible. Even if Nikola could hire someone with Evergreen controlling her funds, this kind of plan would only work with as few people as possible knowing the truth. I wouldn't be surprised if Woodrow was the next on the list to bump off."

Cold sweat formed on Woodrow's forehead.

"You keep talking in circles without any sound logic," Nikola criticized. "You said that the only people who know the truth are in this room. You've proven that Woodrow couldn't have done it. And you've explained how I didn't kill him. Unless you're claiming that companion of yours is the murderer, you have nothing."

"That wouldn't be surprising with his temper," Woodrow chided.

"Woah, hey, rude much?" I growled.

"There is still one more person who knows your little secret. Someone who wouldn't mind killing for your sake. Someone who would go through all this effort if it meant you were safe and secure. Your real father," Kai said.

At first, Nikola widened her eyes, but it didn't take long for the look to fade from her eyes, leaving her gaze downcast.

"My real father?" Nikola frowned.

"Of course. Who else could you trust? Your mother is dead. Your stepfather was a megalomaniac and is also dead. Woodrow, while sympathetic, was still loyal to his former employer." Kai shrugged.

"Her real father is here?" Woodrow asked.

"Why would he be here now after all these years?" Nikola asked.

"You mean why would a caring father show up in his daughter's time of need?" Kai answered.

"Enough. If he was a caring father, why wait until now? Why not save my mother? Why not take me away sooner?" Nikola asked.

There was a pause as Kai took a moment to answer.

"Unfortunately, there is no easy answer," Kai finally said. "Maria probably never told your father about you and Evergreen probably made sure to intercept any connections to your real father. This is evident since Evergreen held onto your letters, after all. He was probably trying to monopolize information."

"Hold on," I interrupted. "If her real father killed Alderheim, who is her real father?" I asked.

"Master Evergreen practically forced the information out of Maria. I managed to overhear that information at the time," Woodrow said.

"Don't bother," Kai interjected. "I already have an idea of who it is."

"How?!" Woodrow asked, astonished.

Nikola's posture changed as she waited in anticipation. Once again, Kai tapped his forehead, taking a moment to think.

"Honestly, I almost found this a little hard to believe. If we are convinced that Nikola's real father is the culprit, then what does the crime scene tell us? One, the culprit has a sweet tooth. Those milk and cookies weren't eaten by Evergreen. Two, we have his address. The letter Nikola wrote was likely addressed to her real father. I can't imagine any other reason Evergreen would confiscate it. The address is in the Arctic Circle, the same as Zed and I received. Lastly, the only place our culprit could escape from in this locked room is the chimney. For most people, that would be a death sentence, but our guy went up the chimney without a second thought. Given all this information, I can only think of one person. The jolly one himself, the patron saint of prostitutes, the one and only Santa Claus!" Kai declared.

The air grew cold.

"Wait a minute," Woodrow interrupted. "When Mr. Evergreen forced a confession out of Maria, the name she gave him was Christopher North."

"A clever alias. The man goes by many different names," Kai answered.

"Either an alias or that was Maria's last effort to flip off

Evergreen," I added.

"In any case, Christopher was probably an alias for Kris Kringle, which is another name he goes by. And the last name North was probably to the North Pole, his home," Kai answered.

Nikola slowly shook her head.

"Not only are you claiming that I had a hand in my stepfather's demise, but now you're claiming that my real father is actually Santa Claus? I assume you have some proof to go along with your theory crafting?" Nikola asked.

Obviously, we have proof, I thought as I glanced at Kai. However, to my dismay, Kai only stroked his chin.

"Kai, what are you waiting for? Answer her," I said.

"Unfortunately, I can't," Kai admitted. "A lot of the evidence is circumstantial at best. And even if we got Henry to testify, it would be his word against hers. The only thing I am certain we can prove is that she isn't Alderheim's daughter. Not that it matters."

"What do you mean? If we prove she isn't his daughter, then she gets nothing," I said.

"Theoretically, but if Evergreen's will were to suddenly turn up," Kai said.

"He could've left everything for the person he loved like a daughter," Nikola added.

"You and I both know Evergreen would never do that," Kai refuted.

"Doesn't matter what you or I think. It would just need to be believed by the court," Nikola said.

"We could prove that it was a forgery," I argued.

"I doubt that," Nikola dismissed. "If someone went to great lengths to forge a will, chances are they spent hours reviewing documents and practicing their penmanship to match their victim. That would make it almost impossible to spot the difference."

"Which would explain the other reason the culprit went rummaging through Evergreen's files," I said.

"That would only be an issue if we believe in Kai's ridiculous theory," Nikola finished.

"Good news, Henry, you won't be murdered next," Kai reassured the butler.

"Gee thanks," Woodrow said.

Pleased with herself, Nikola moved towards the door.

"Well, this was entertaining, but if there is nothing else then I'll be taking my leave," she said, waving her hand.

"Well played," Kai said. "Though you didn't account for the one overlooked detail."

"Bluffing won't help," Nikola said as she kept walking.

"Am I? What if I told you I could easily sabotage this plan of yours?" Kai declared.

Rolling her eyes, Nikola turned around.

"Fine, if you wish to embarrass yourself further. What is it?" she asked.

"All we need to do is capture Santa Claus and prove that he is your real father. Once we do that, proving everything else would be simple enough."

"Is that the best you could come up with, Detective?" she said, the disappointment was evident in Nikola's voice. "And here I thought you had a trick up your sleeve. But your grand plan is to catch a myth. Even if we believe your theory, it would be pointless, as my 'real father' would've been long gone by now," Nikola said.

"Oh, really?" Kai gave a sly grin.

A trace of concern flashed before the young woman's face. She eyed him carefully, unsure of what he was planning.

"That's too bad," Kai continued. "There is only one way to stop you now."

"What, send the authorities on a wild goose chase after a legend?" Nikola asked sarcastically.

"No," Kai said and then he snapped his fingers.

Suddenly, a revolver appeared in Kai's hand and he pointed it straight at Nikola.

"If I kill you right now, this whole charade comes to an end," Kai said, smiling.

"Look here you-," Woodrow attempted to get in the middle, but I quickly restrained him by pinning him to the ground. I wasn't sure what was going through Kai's mind, but I could tell by the fire in his eyes he hadn't given up yet.

"Let's leave those two to their conversation," I said.

"This is it? You think killing me will justify your crazy idea?" Nikola said.

"Nothing personal, it's just business. If I let this murderer go free, this would seriously damage my reputation. Just think of this as me putting an end to your family tragedy," Kai said.

Nikola tried to maintain her poker face, but staring down the barrel of a gun makes that difficult for anyone. She took a step back toward the door. Kai snapped his fingers.

"Got it," I said as my human-self split off and dashed in front of the door.

"There are two of you?" Nikola asked.

I smiled, blocking her only exit.

"What are you?" Woodrow asked as my beast-self kept him pinned down.

"You've got nowhere to go," Kai said.

"You know this is pointless, right?" Nikola said.

Kai cocked back the hammer of the gun.

"Are you really going to kill me?" Nikola pleaded.

A wicked grin was plastered on Kai's face.

"Are you expecting me to beg?" Nikola said.

Kai's grin broadened into a sinister smile.

"Please…" Nikola begged.

Raising his eyebrow, Kai lowered his gun.

"Tell you what," Kai said. "Answer this question and I'll let you off."

Nikola hesitantly nodded her head.

"How does one catch the elusive myth, Saint Nick?" Kai asked.

"What?" Nikola stammered.

"Did I stutter?" Kai affirmed.

"That isn't possible," Nikola shot back.

Kai let out a laugh.

"I thought you might say that," he said. "Let me give you a piece of advice."

Kai took his index finger and tapped his forehead several times.

"Don't think of it as how to catch a myth."

Without a moment of hesitation, Kai pulled the trigger and the gun roared like thunder.

Act III

Chapter XVI

As I held the gun in my hands, I felt everyone's eyes on me. Henry, Nikola, and the two Zeds stared in anticipation. I tapped my forehead.

"Don't think of it as how to catch a myth," I said.

I winked as I pulled the trigger. The bullet went speeding directly towards Nikola's head. In an instant, the bullet vanished in a flash of red, white, and a hint of green. Nikola, though unharmed, collapsed.

"It's how you catch a protective father," I continued.

The air grew cold as seconds passed. It felt like time slowed to a screeching halt. Suddenly, a gust of wind howled like a raging storm.

"Answer: Use their kid as bait," I said, smiling.

The howling winds died down, but the air was still filled with hostility. A hulking figure greeted us standing over six feet in a red fur coat who carried a massive brown sack at his side.

The two Zeds gawked at the massive figure before us. I continued to smile as I finally managed to draw out the elusive figure.

"I presume you're the mastermind behind today's events," I said casually. "Ah, but where are my manners? What should I call you? Santa? Mr. Claus? Father Christmas? Saint Nick? Or maybe Christopher North? Though I believe murderer is far more appropriate," I mocked.

"You'd better watch out," the hulking mass threatened.

"It was you this entire time," Woodrow said in awe.

Beast-Zed was too stunned to keep the butler pinned. I clapped my hands.

"Okay that's enough gawking. It's time to get down to business. It was you, Mr. Claus, that sent me the letter warning me away." I said.

"HO, HO, HO! If it was, you'd be a naughty boy for ignoring my warning," Santa laughed.

"Yeah, so what? You're gonna give me a face full of coal like you did Evergreen?" I rebuked.

"Wait," Woodrow interrupted. "I don't understand. Why now? After all these years, why did you choose now to look after Nikola?" Woodrow asked.

The Jolly One wouldn't even look in Woodrow's direction. Instead, the hulking mass kept his eyes fixed on me. Despite his jovial tone, there was an air of unease surrounding him.

"As I thought, you didn't know," I said.

Santa remained silent.

"I guess after the Christmas Eve tryst, Maria didn't tell you about the gift you had given her that day."

The Jolly One arched a brow.

"It wasn't that hard," I continued. "When I found out Nikola's birthday was in September, all I had to do was count backwards. Plus, Evergreen being the control freak that he was, Christmas Eve was the only time you'd be able to cross paths with Maria."

"I see a lot of faces every year. You can't expect me to

remember every single one," Santa said.

"Oh, really? You expect me to believe the guy in charge of who's been naughty or nice forgot Maria Swan, the famed actress who was once a national sensation? Surely, you can make a better excuse than that," I teased.

Woodrow remained unconvinced and the butler came in between the two of us.

"But that doesn't explain his actions. Why this whole scheme? Why not just take Maria away if you really cared for her? Better yet, why didn't you take Nikola away when you learned she was your daughter?"

Despite Woodrow's mounting questions, Santa remained silent.

"Unfortunately," I said, "the answer isn't a favorable one, He's married. And I bet Mrs. Claus wouldn't be happy about your infidelity."

"If he cared about his marriage so much, then why get involved with Maria just to abandon her?" Woodrow probed.

"I'm curious about that as well," Zed mentioned.

"So how was it done, ol' boy? Let me guess, was it under the mistletoe?" I grinned.

Despite my provocations, Santa only smiled at me. It was such an unexpected reaction that I felt a bead of cold sweat on my brow. Then his smile then morphed into melancholy.

"I've been around for a long time," Santa finally said. "Some would call it a curse, and maybe it is, being forced to watch the world change and evolve as you remain the same. But when you've been around as long as I have, you only really remember people like Maria. Smart, vibrant, elegant, and so full of life. The world could be ending tomorrow but she would insist that the show must go on. It really was breathtaking to watch her perform. You could imagine my surprise when she announced her retirement. I suppose even the most beautiful flower has to wilt eventually. I never fully understood that until I saw it for myself."

"You were a fan of hers," I added.

"I managed to catch a few of her shows from time to time," Santa continued. "When I finally met her, she was turning into a husk of her former self. Completely miserable. And it was all because of that man."

Santa's face soured and the air too grew tense with hostility. Beast-Zed was quick to brandish his claws, but I signaled him to stand down. After a moment, Santa relaxed and looked up towards the ceiling.

"All she wanted was one night to forget her problems. To feel alive again, to feel free if only for one night. Who would've thought an unexpected miracle would've transpired that night?"

"You really didn't know the result of your one-night stand?" I asked.

"It shouldn't have been possible," Santa remarked.

I didn't understand what he was getting at. Noticing my befuddlement, the Jolly One let out a big laugh.

"I suppose there are things even you don't know," Santa said.

"Mind sharing with the class, then?" I asked.

"I've lived for eons, you fool. Do you think this is the first time I've been around? For decades, I thought it was impossible. A price for this immortality," Santa said.

Zed's eyes lit up upon realization.

"Nikola isn't just your only daughter, she's your only child. Your only legacy," I said.

"That's why you never knew about Nikola. She shouldn't

have-" Zed explained.

"But she does," Santa interrupted.

"Wait a minute," I said. "If this is true, how did you learn about Nikola? Why did you formally meet with Evergreen?"

Santa merely smiled at my questions. It was irritating that he knew I hadn't figured it out.

"Normally," Santa continued. "I admire your pursuit of the truth. You've done quite a lot of good with that attitude. However, you made one mistake that I can't overlook."

Once again the air grew tense. When the smile Santa wore evaporated, I instinctively tightened the grip on my gun. The two Zeds brandished their teeth and claws, waiting to pounce.

"That mistake was betting on my daughter's life!" Santa exclaimed.

Instantly, he charged at us like a freight train. Beast-Zed and I quickly split up to avoid the attack. Santa kept going until he crashed into a wall.

"I think we made him mad," I said.

"We?" Beast-Zed growled.

"You were the one that pulled a gun on his daughter!" Human-Zed complained from across the room.

"I don't need both of you echoing in my ear," I groaned.

In the distance, the Jolly One rose from the hole in the wall, ready to charge again. We took our fighting stance.

"This was your idea, so what's the plan?" Beast-Zed growled.

"Dispel your clone and take the girl out of here," I whispered.

Beast-Zed looked surprised. "Are you nuts? This is THE Santa Clause," he argued.

"Listen," I said, "he doesn't really care about us. What he really cares about is his daughter. So as long as we have Nikola, Murder Claus will have to play by our rules. So, take her and run, and don't let her go."

Beast-Zed looked conflicted, but sensing there was no time to argue, human-Zed ran for the unconscious Nikola.

"I hope you know what you are doing," Beast-Zed said as he morphed into a shadow returning to Zed.

"Do you really think I'll let you escape?" Santa said, aiming for Zed.

With little time to spare, I shot a volley of gunfire at the Christmas icon. Somehow, the big guy managed to dodge the barrage of bullets. Ignoring me, Santa headed straight for Zed. Zed's only focus was on the girl in front of him. Stopping to collect her, Zed knelt down. Unbeknownst to him, Santa was about to strike. Just as the mad Claus was going to connect, my knife flew toward his neck. Sensing the danger, Santa took a step back and avoided the attack. In that brief window, Zed managed to escape with Nikola over his shoulder.

"You know you're only delaying the inevitable," Santa said.

"We'll see about that," I said as I put on a pair of gloves.

I fired several shots, but in the next moment a gust of wind redirected the bullets right back at me. I quickly snapped my fingers. The Jolly One looked my way, only to find that I had disappeared from sight. Confused, Santa looked around.

"Over here!" I shouted from behind. Santa turned around as I tried to cut him from behind. Santa was barely able to dodge the blow. I grazed his beard, splitting a few hairs off. Not wanting to give him a moment to breathe, I threw my knife. The Jolly One ducked down and charged at me.

As soon as he approached, Santa slammed his fist toward me. The incredible force caused the ground to quake and produced a cloud of dust. The winter air channeled through the fireplace and caused the dust cloud to disperse. Much to his chagrin, Santa realized I had disappeared again. But not for long. I greeted him with a punch to the back of the head. The old man staggered forward and then immediately retaliated by striking with a back fist. I ducked down to avoid the strike and kicked him sharply behind his knees. Santa went tumbling. Capitalizing on the advantage, I stood up and placed my knife to his throat.

"What's wrong? Getting slow in your old age?" I mocked.

"You impudent little..." Santa said as the frigid air grew turbulent.

A windstorm swirled, and the raging winds threw me from Santa's back. Everything in the room blew around in a frenzy. Even Woodrow, who had been hiding behind the desk, was sent flying through the air. Barely able to see, I could hear the butler's screams grow louder until we collided in the air. Growing tired of being a ragdoll, I grabbed onto Woodrow as I stabbed my knife into the ground to keep us in place in the howling winds. Eventually, the winds died down and Woodrow and I tried to catch our breath.

"You have my thanks," Woodrow said.

I nodded and saw Santa holding his bag. From inside it, he drew out a giant candy cane.

"That reminds me, I still owe Woodrow for his part in all of this," Santa menaced.

I felt Woodrow quiver in fear beside me. The big man lunged at the butler, swinging his candy cane. Protecting Woodrow, I used my knife and clashed with the mad Claus. I was struggling to hold the big guy in place, and he kept slowly pushing me back.

"I believe that's twice I owe you," Woodrow said.

"You can pay me back by getting out of my way!" I replied.

With no hesitation, Woodrow ran towards the door. As I watched the butler leave, my vision started to blur.

Damn, not now.

"I can always find him later," Santa remarked.

I didn't have the energy to respond. Instead, I let out a loud yawn. With my guard down, Santa grabbed me by the neck and choke-slammed me. I gasped for air after the wind was knocked out of me. Santa raised the cane, ready to cave in my skull. I fired a quick shot in vain as Santa tilted his head to avoid the bullet. Before I could fire again the cane slammed down.

"What?" the Jolly One said, surprised.

My body had disappeared.

"Up here," I said.

I prepared to land a dropkick on my foe. However, my body was quickly hooked in by the candy cane. Changing my trajectory, I was swung head-first into the ground like a hammer.

Sensing immediate danger, I threw my knife in a panic. I aimed for Santa's blind spot behind him. I quickly retreated behind him, ready to strike, but Santa spun the candy cane like a bo staff. He swung the cane overhead and caught me in the hook. Using the momentum, I was launched into the wall. Pain overtook me as I collapsed to the ground.

"Now I understand," Santa continued. "Your Grace is teleportation! That would explain why you're so hard to pin down. However, there's a limit to it. You can only go where your knife or gun fires, correct?"

"Something like that," I struggled to say.

He was half-right. My Grace, called Rune displacement, is like teleportation. As long as my rune is on the object or person, I can teleport, or displace it. I can also switch objects around as long as my rune is placed on them. My signature knife, Vorator, and my revolver, Scarlet Hiro, have my runes inscribed on them, as do each of my bullets. I usually wear gloves to make it easier to place my runes, but I have other ways as well.

There are drawbacks though, the more I use my grace the more mana I use, which can make me very tired. Also, the heavier the object the more mana I burn. However, in order to mitigate this problem, Vorator siphons the energy from anybody it cuts or stabs, and I can mimic their special features such as other Graces or certain physical traits. However, the effects only last for a limited time.

"No matter. I doubt you can keep this up for much longer." Santa said.

Bingo, I thought.

"Oh really, care to find out?" I taunted.

Santa charged at me and I threw my knife. Santa, as expected, spun around and swung his candy cane to hook me in from behind. This time, all he caught was empty air. Before he realized why, I gave him a sharp punch to the kidneys. Staggering forward, the old man lunged the cane behind me. Before I was pulled in, I displaced myself toward my knife in the wall. Retrieving my blade, I dashed at Santa, preparing to slash him. The old man blocked my attack with his candy cane.

"Just because you have a basic understanding of my Grace doesn't mean it's easy to predict," I argued.

Despite my boast, I was in a terrible position. Using rune displacement so much was draining my mana pool, and I had a hard time stifling my yawns.

I just need to cut him once.

Despite everything going on, I noticed Saint Nick kept stealing glances at the door.

Of course! He's in a hurry too, I thought.

"Worried about your daughter? Fret not, Zed's taking good care of her," I taunted.

"Hah! You think I'm worried about that mutt? Oh, I have a special plan for him," Santa threatened.

The old man's self-assured smile gave me a temporary pause.

"What are you talking about?" I asked.

"For a detective, you sure are slow!"

"Oh, shut up!" I yelled.

"Hmph, enough, let's finish this," Santa declared.

"Fine by me," I agreed.

Both of us took a step back as we readied ourselves. Winter air gathered around Santa as he prepared his final strike. I didn't want to be outdone, so I tapped into my mana. My idea was risky, but I wasn't left with many options. Focusing, I felt a flurry of green sparks tingle around me. I gathered the energy and focused it on Vorator. The blade glowed green as it began to grow and extend. The length of the blade was limited due to my exhaustion, but it was sufficient. Our eyes met as we took our stance. In the next instant, our war cries echoed in the room and we dashed towards each other. Our weapons collided, pushing us back and forth. Neither one of us were willing to surrender. The green energy surrounding my blade flared up like a power saw chipping away at Santa's candy cane.

"Looks like I've won."

Chapter XVII

As the situation unfolded, I couldn't help but wonder if we were still the good guys in this scenario. I had to push my moral questions aside though, because I was clueless about what to do next. *Where am I going?*

Running through the halls, the floor above me shook violently. One of the ceiling lights fell down in my path. Without stopping, I jumped over it.

"Kai must be giving it his all," I said.

I couldn't leave the manor because of the blizzard outside. Still running, I passed by what appeared to be one of the living rooms. Running in my human form was a bit taxing. I double-checked to ensure I wasn't followed and laid Nikola on the couch. It was surprising the girl had remained unconscious the whole time. I sat next to Nikola and took a minute to weigh my options. Before I could come up with anything, the floor overhead exploded with the sounds of crashing bodies and gunshots.

I hope Kai doesn't run out of steam before we think of a counterattack.

That thought only lasted for a second, then my animal instincts kicked in, warning me of what was to come. I jumped out of my seat, ready to take on any threat. One of the maids appeared in the doorway.

"Oh, hey Elizabeth," I said, lowering my guard slightly.

Elizabeth didn't respond, she just stared at me blankly. I wasn't sure what was happening, but I knew something was amiss.

"Mama…" Nikola muttered in her sleep.

Her comment was enough to take my eyes off the maid. I attempted to check on the poor girl, but that was until I felt a sudden punch to the face, which sent me flying across the room.

"What the heck was that for?" I groaned.

Elizabeth ignored me and went straight for Nikola on the couch. As the goat maid reached out to grab the girl, my hand wrapped around Elizabeth's. The hand was coming out of my shadow, holding on to the maid. Emerging from the pool of darkness, my furry beast-self was standing on two legs, eyes glowing above teeth sharp enough to chew through bone.

"That wasn't very nice," my beast-self growled.

Not wasting a moment, Elizabeth pulled my beast-self's arm in to headbutt me. I barely avoided her horns when our foreheads clashed. After our heads collided, I took a step back, disoriented. But Elizabeth gave me no chance to breathe, as she threw a roundhouse kick and a few jabs my way. I kept my guard up, blocking each strike. Meanwhile, my human-self ran past us to retrieve Nikola. After I moved the girl a safe distance away, my beast-self brandished his claws and took several swipes at Elizabeth. She quickly backed away, dodging the first slash, grazing her outfit. Elizabeth twirled away elegantly, dodging each strike. In the background, I gazed at my beast-self and Elizabeth engaged in battle.

"This doesn't make any sense," I said. "Why are you attacking me? Are you working for Santa?" I asked.

Elizabeth remained silent as she kept on fighting. My beast-self continued his attacks, but each one was deftly avoided and countered. When I threw a right hook, Elizabeth ducked and kicked me in the ribs. Luckily, I braced myself and grabbed her leg, ready to capitalize. She quickly performed a backflip, swinging her free leg up and connecting with my beast's chin. The force of the blow caused him to release Elizabeth from his grasp. I got a good look at Elizabeth's eyes during the attack. They looked vacant, with no color in them. As she landed, the goat maid looked in my direction and dashed towards my human-self as I held Nikola in my arms.

Meanwhile, my beast-self grew increasingly upset at the devolving situation. Blinded by rage, he grabbed the couch and threw it in our direction. Surprised, I leaped out of the way, ensuring not to drop Nikola. The couch hit Elizabeth, and she crashed into the wall.

"Watch where you're attacking, you almost hit the girl!" I yelled.

"Why are you still here? Kai said to run!" my beast-self growled.

"I know, but something doesn't make sense-"

Before I could finish my sentence, Elizabeth kicked off the couch that had been pinning her down. A spinning kick in my direction followed. I used my free arm to block it, but it still pushed me back a few inches. Elizabeth continued her onslaught until my beast-self tackled her to the ground.

"Run!" he roared.

As I was about to leave, I hesitated when I noticed a trace of black lines on the floor that led around the corner. I recognized them. They could explain Elizabeth's bizarre behavior. I conjured up my shadow from the ground as it began to morph. My shadow formed into a dog. The dog, my hound-self, shook its fur followed by stretching his back.

Allow me to explain, my Grace is called Gatekeeper, which allows me to split myself into three, though we can't share the same form at one time. Each operates autonomously and we can share thoughts. My other selves have different personality types. My beast self is the most aggressive one, always leaning towards violence. Hound form is the most dog-like, so he's more playful. My human side is typically the most rational. However, when one of my forms die, some of the damage is passed on to those that remain, which can be a significant blow to my mana pool. That makes it harder to summon another form for a limited time.

With my hound-self fully aware of the situation, he followed the lines on the ground. There was only one thing that could've created those black lines. I followed along as we turned the corner to see the second maid.

"Mary," I barked.

The marionette stared at us with those creepy eyes. Mary had used her shadow theater to possess Elizabeth into attacking me. This explained why Elizabeth didn't react to any pain while she fought. My hound-self charged at the doll. The doll twirled away like a spinning top, avoiding us.

This is annoying.

Even though the doll was frail, it was still agile as it danced around us. Because I was carrying an unconscious woman, my movement was hampered. Eventually, Mary struck a pose and stood in the center of the room. My hound-self pounced towards the doll. Suddenly, my beast-self came crashing in through the wall, colliding into my hound-self in the process.

I turned to see Elizabeth mirroring Mary's posture.

"That's it, I'm going to rip you apart," my beast-self roared.

"Stop, Elizabeth is just the puppet. We need to stop the doll," I pleaded.

"Fat chance, I can't even get near her," my hound-self barked.

Losing patience, my beast-self made a beeline for Mary. Surprisingly, instead of protecting her host, Elizabeth went straight for Nikola. Sensing my danger, my beast-self changed his direction towards me. Elizabeth attempted to kick him, but she was quickly intercepted by my beast-self. Grabbing her leg, my beast-self spun the maid around and tossed her at Mary.

Unfortunately, Mary was able to avoid the flying Elizabeth and the possessed maid performed mid-air roll to land on her feet. The maids gathered as they mirrored each other's fighting stance.

"We're not gonna get anywhere near the doll at this rate. Elizabeth's defense is too good," my hound-self barked.

"I can't fight like this. Either ditch the girl and let me loose or we have to run," my beast-self growled.

"Maybe we have a third option," I said.

Thinking quickly, I came up with a plan and projected the thoughts to my other selves. After a few seconds, Elizabeth dashed towards us, ready to fight. However, as she was about to throw the first punch, both maids held still, as my beast-self had a claw to Nikola's throat.

As I thought. Mary's prime objective is to keep Nikola safe. I wasn't a fan of the idea, but desperate times call for desperate measures.

"That's right. If you don't want us to slice off your mistress's head, I suggest you back off nice and slow," I demanded.

Me, myself, and I slowly backed away from the situation, making sure not to take our eyes off the maids. This process went on for a while until the maids decided to retreat. I didn't understand until I felt the air grow cold and the hairs on my neck stood up. I thought I had bumped into the wall, but when I turned around, I saw the hulking mass of Santa Claus.

"There you are," Santa said.

Before my human-self could react, we heard a loud crunch as my human body went flying through the hall, slamming through the walls as he went. Immediately, my beast-self and I collapsed to the ground, causing us to drop Nikola.

Dazed, my thoughts swirled. My heart was beating erratically and my body screamed with pain. I felt both my bodies shake violently. I didn't understand what was happening until I finally realized that monster had killed one of me with a single blow.

My beast-self was panting and struggling to breathe as he desperately tried to reach out for Nikola. Santa stepped on his hand and raised his other leg, ready to slam his foot on my beast-self's head. Before the blow struck, I dispelled my beast clone, turning him back into an inky black shadow as he returned to me. I had no choice. If I lost both my figures, I would've become completely immobile from the damage suffered. Fighting through the pain and taking advantage of the distraction, I bit down on Nikola's shirt collar and dragged her away. As I tried to escape, I heard footsteps hasten in my direction. Before I could see who was speeding towards me, I felt a sharp kick to the ribs. Nikola and I skidded across the floor. Elizabeth had re-entered the fray. It was hard to catch my breath, but I still forced myself to stand up on my own four feet.

"How the hell did you get past Kai?" I barked.

"The same way I just got past you," Santa said, brandishing his boxing glove.

"Liar," I snapped.

"Believe it or not, your master is not coming to help. But I'll strike a deal with you. Give up my daughter and I'll let you live," Santa said.

Saint Nick and Elizabeth stared me down menacingly. I considered his choice for a moment.

There's no way I can get past both of these titans at the same time. I need some time to heal.

My thoughts were racing as I tried to figure a way out of that mess.

"I can tell by your eyes that you have no intention of surrendering. However, I urge you to put an end to this drawn-out game and walk away. Kai isn't here to save you. You don't have a reason to fight anymore," Santa said, trying to convince me.

I looked at Nikola and considered it.

He's right. She's been a pain since we arrived. Kai can't be dead, but should I keep risking my life for this?

Then I remembered Kai's words.

"Liar," I said. Santa was silent. "I also know Nikola's secret. You'd never let me just walk away."

Disappointed, Santa shook his head.

"Then I'm afraid you leave me no other choice," the man said as he grabbed me by the throat. "It's time to put this dog down."

I barely had any energy left to struggle against his tightening grip. I tried biting Santa's hand, but it was all for naught. A glove protected his hand. Staring into this madman's eyes, memories replayed in my mind. Some I wish I had forgotten. Others I wished I could change. I wondered,

Is this what it feels like to die?

Chapter XVIII

F*ifteen minutes earlier.*

I felt my heels being pushed back inch by inch. As Santa let out his mad laughter, I gritted my teeth and fended off his candy cane with my blade.

"Looks like I've won," Santa declared.

I just need one clean cut. Come on, come on!

As if it was responding to my thoughts, my blade began to eat through the candy cane. The jolly man's laugh came to a screeching halt as his weapon was sliced clean through. Once the candy cane was no longer a threat, I followed up with a roundhouse kick. The old man jumped back, narrowly avoiding my strike. I charged at him, swinging my knife like a madman.

"Boxing gloves, now!" Santa yelled out.

In the corner, two gloves shot out of the brown bag and headed directly toward Santa. Once the gloves were on Santa's hands, he went on the offensive. Santa ducked as he came rushing towards me, firing off a quick jab to the face. I took half a step back to dodge the punch. While I managed to evade it, the force of the air moving past me left a small cut on my cheek.

Did he get stronger?

Alarmed, I retreated a few more steps back.

"What's wrong? You seem surprised," Santa said.

Before I could respond, the old man rushed at me with a flurry of punches. Once again, I was backed into a corner and had to concentrate solely on evasion. It was clear now that both Santa's punching speed and strength had increased significantly. Blocking seemed like a terrible idea, so I was forced to evade his attacks.

As the fight went on, I continued to be patient. When Santa threw a wide right hook, I avoided it completely and drew my Scarlet Hiro with my left hand. Just before I pulled the trigger, Santa's left fist shot out and knocked my gun away. My left hand went numb, but I gritted through it and dashed at the man head-first. Balling my right hand into a fist, I threw a straight punch at the old man's face, but Santa intercepted it with his own punch. The force of our attacks colliding released a shockwave throughout the room. Thankfully, Santa's fist collided with my knife instead of my hand.

"Finally," I smiled.

All I needed was for Vorator to rip through the glove to land a decisive cut.

FEED!

Green sparks began to form as the knife gathered energy, but the energy quickly fizzled out.

"What?!" I exclaimed.

"You seem confused," Santa said. "I figured you were up to something with this butter knife, so I made sure my gloves were knife-proof."

"Shit," I swore.

"I believe it's time to bring this fight to a close," Santa declared.

Santa took a deep breath and then a surge of power radiated from his fist. Using it, he pushed me back. I tried using both arms to push back, but the old man quickly gained momentum and his fist shot me through the air like a cannon.

"Have a nice flight," he said as my body went flying through a wall.

The old man laughed as I crashed down.

"Time to put that mutt in the ground," the old man said.

Turning away from me, I tried to reach my hand out. It was useless. I felt immense pain and exhaustion all over my body. I was well past my limit. Everything faded to black.

Kai.... Kai, Kai.

"KAI!"

I jolted awake.

"You're alive, right?" the voice asked.

Woodrow was pulling rubble off me. After a few minutes, he helped me to my feet.

"What are you doing here?" I asked.

"I'm returning the favor. You saved my life twice, the least I can do is help you on your feet," Woodrow answered.

"The old man really got me good," I said.

"I heard," Woodrow said.

While that black-out nap did me some good, I was still weary from the fight. I grabbed a flask from my breast pocket and started drinking.

"Drowning your sorrows already?" Woodrow quipped.

"Not exactly," I continued. "This is just an energy drink of my own special blend."

It took a few seconds to kick in and it didn't heal my damage, but that wasn't an immediate problem.

"Seems like you're already looking better," Woodrow said.

"Yes, yes. Now bring me up to speed. What did I miss while I was out?" I asked, looking around the room.

"Not much time has elapsed since your battle. After your defeat, Santa ran out," Woodrow explained.

Looking for Nikola I'd bet, which means he's still here.

"What's this?" I asked, picking up a hand-sized box.

"A jack-in-the-box. Mr. Evergreen had a habit of collecting them," Woodrow explained.

I kept inspecting the ground, canvassing the area.

"Are you sure you want to waste time here?" Woodrow continued. "I'm afraid your partner may be on his last legs."

"Santa found him?" I asked.

"Yes, but he's not alone, I can lead the way."

"No, that won't be necessary. But you can help in a different way." I quickly found what I was looking for.

"How?" Woodrow asked.

"Shake my hand," I demanded.

Woodrow stared at me tentatively but held onto my hand without a fuss.

"Thank you for coming to my aid," I said.

"You're welcome-ow!" Woodrow cried out when I cut into the back of his hand. "Apologies Henry, but you can consider us even after this," I said as I ran out of the room.

Feed.

On command, green sparks roared out from Vorator as Woodrow's blood was slowly being devoured. I felt my knife imbuing me with energy as my ears grew longer. With my mana pool restored, there was only one thing left to do. I snapped my fingers.

"It's time to put this dog down," Santa said as he arched his arm back. The punch was thrown straight at Zed as he struggled to break free.

Then Zed suddenly disappeared from Santa's grasp, causing his punch to only hit the air. Flabbergasted, the old man looked beneath him and saw me slide past him to grab Nikola.

"Phew, seems like I made it on time," I said.

"Sheesh, what took you so long?" Zed wheezed.

"Apologies, I got held up," I answered. "Good job protecting the princess," I said, patting Zed on the head.

"Well, well, well, I thought you were down for the count!" Santa clapped his hands and continued, "I guess this makes things even."

"Even?" I asked.

Then I heard rapid footsteps heading in my direction. Before I could react, Zed bit down on the cuff of my shirt and pulled me to the side. A roundhouse kick to the back of the head whizzed by. I saw my attacker was Elizabeth. As her foot flew by, I saw her eyes were blank, with no color in them.

"Careful, the doll is pulling her strings," Zed informed.

"The vacant eyes were a dead giveaway," I said.

"I tried multiple times to pin down the doll, but each time Elizabeth got in the way," Zed explained.

"Then multiply and hunt the doll down," I said.

"I had to dispel my clones after Murder Claus killed one of them,"

Zed won't be able to clone himself for a while, I thought.

"Guess there is only one thing left to do," I said as I brandished my knife.

Zed growled as he was ready to attack. Elizabeth and Santa slowly approached. I gripped Vorator, ready to make a move as Santa cracked his knuckles. Just as a clash seemed imminent...

"See ya!"

"Later!"

Zed and I exclaimed as we made a hasty retreat, while our sudden escape left our enemies dumbfounded.

"Get back here!" Santa yelled as he and Elizabeth gave chase.

Zed and I were sprinting down the hall with Nikola on my companion's back.

"Please tell me you have a real plan," Zed said.

"I told you, as long as we have Nikola, we control the tide of battle," I answered.

"Then what? We can't keep running forever," Zed rebuked.

"Still working on that part," I admitted.

The two of us ran until we reached a crossroads.

"Split up," I ordered.

"What about you?" Zed asked.

"Just do it, trust me."

Without hesitation, Zed turned left and I turned right. Our pursuers soon caught up. Elizabeth didn't even slow down as she followed right behind Zed. She was tailing him since he was carrying Nikola. Conversely, Santa stopped and weighed his options. After a moment, he followed my direction. Can't say I was surprised.

"Come now, you didn't think I'd fall for that split-up routine," Santa taunted.

I kept silent and threw my knife at him. Santa used his glove to block, knocking the projectile back in my direction. I caught the blade with ease and pulled out my gun. I fired a few shots. Santa was dashing towards me, but he still avoided every shot. Each bullet that got close to Santa vanished into a puff of snow. I held my ground and kept firing. Through the suppressing fire, I saw Zed in the distance. He was running for his life, trying to avoid the possessed maid at all costs. In the midst of my distraction, I almost didn't notice how quickly Santa closed the distance between us. He threw a haymaker that I managed by ducking down and rolling. The old man was persistent though, and he kept rushing at me.

"What's wrong, worried about Zed?" Santa taunted.

Fully focused, I ignored him and evaded his blows.

"Your plan was so easy to read," Santa said. "You wanted both of us to chase after your little pet so you could trick us with your Grace. You were going to teleport him away and escape."

A trace of concern must have shown on my face.

"Ha, I was right," Santa laughed. "Tell me, what will you do? You can't defeat me and your partner is about to be caught," Santa mocked as he threw another haymaker.

Now!

Waiting for this moment, I pulled out Vorator and used the blade to block the oncoming attack. Once again, our attacks clashed and I was being pushed back. I used my free hand to grab Santa's glove to support my blade, pushing back. However, the attempt was fruitless.

"Seems like the odds are stacked against you," Santa mentioned.

"Well," I finally said, "then we should even those odds!"

Santa was taken aback, but before he could respond, a burst of flames erupted from the corridor. At the same time, Elizabeth collapsed dead in her tracks. Noticing the sudden events, the old man's jaw dropped.

"How did you-"

"Later!" I said as I vanished before Santa's eyes.

I returned to running side by side with Zed.

"What was that all about?" Zed asked.

"I called in a favor, now keep moving," I answered.

We kept on running for a while. As we ran, Zed and I took a moment to look at our surroundings. That's when we noticed something.

"Kai," Zed called out.

"Yeah, we're not imagining it," I said.

Our environment hadn't changed and now we were being pulled backwards by some force.

"We're not going anywhere," Zed and I said in unison.

Looking behind us, we saw Santa Claus using his giant bag of gifts as a vacuum that was sucking us in. I pulled out Scarlet Hiro and tried to return fire at our assailant. Before the bullets could find their target, each was sucked directly into the bag.

Not good.

The suction grew stronger and debris flew around us. Coffee tables, chairs, and lamps all came in our direction. I couldn't displace us out of there, as the damage from the last bout had taken its toll. Zed also looked exhausted. I needed to conserve as much mana as possible. I tried blasting away the incoming furniture while Zed tried to sidestep and dodge. Unfortunately, Zed tripped over a lamp that flew towards us.

"No, wait!" Zed cried out.

The unconscious Nikola fell to the ground along with Zed. Seeing her being pulled towards the bag, I dove after her, but she was slipping further out of reach. In desperation, I threw my knife to close the distance between her and me. I displaced myself to Vorator and held out my hand. I was inches away as I tried to reach out and grab her. Despite my efforts, Nikola vanished into the bag.

"Game over, boys!" the old man said with a hearty laugh.

Zed and I quickly moved into position, ready to attack.

Vorator glowed a dark green, ready to feed. Zed brandished both his fangs and claws, ready to rip Santa to shreds.

"Better luck next time. MERRY CHRISTMAS!" Santa bellowed.

Zed and I pounced in unison. We were seconds away when he touched his nose. A gust of wind roared and blew past us and surrounded the old man, which sent Zed and I flying. As the wind began to die down, an empty hallway greeted us. Nikola and Santa Claus were nowhere in sight.

Chapter XIX

Nothing. Absolutely nothing. Zed and I stared at an empty hallway devoid of Saint Nick and Nikola.

"Damn it," I yelled, slamming my fist on the ground. "Without the girl we have nothing, no leverage, no proof, and no reason for him to stay."

"Do we know where he's heading?" Zed asked.

I closed my eyes as I cupped my hands to my ears. Thanks to Woodrow, I was able to borrow his Grace. I stayed quiet and listened throughout the whole building. I heard a lot of walking and talking from the guests on the ground floor. The constant clutter of random noises gave me a headache. I deepened my focus and heard howling winds, jingle bells, and the old man's jolly laughter.

"Ho, ho, ho!"

"Gotcha," I said.

"Zed, how long till you can make your forms again?" I asked.

"Maybe a few more minutes," Zed said.

I tossed my flask at Zed.

"Drink up, I need you at full energy," I ordered.

"I never liked the taste of these," Zed groaned.

As Zed drank, I heard footsteps slowly approaching us. Reacting, I aimed my gun, ready to pull the trigger.

"Woah, woah, is that any way to treat a friend?" Joe said.

"Oh, it's just you," I said, lowering my gun.

"What are you doing here?" Zed asked.

"Doing you guys a favor," Joe added.

"Nevermind that, we gotta start moving. Zed, how are you feeling?" I asked.

"Not quite one hundred percent, but well enough," Zed answered.

"Good. Turner, you hold down the fort in case we need backup," I ordered.

"Fine, but what are you going to do?" Joe asked.

I smiled as I headed towards a window, grabbing Zed.

"Wait, Kai, are you-" Zed started.

"Yes," I cut him off.

"Isn't there another way we can do this?"

"Nope."

"At least give me a minute."

"You got three."

"Thanks."

"Seconds."

"Wait, wait, wait," Zed pleaded.

Ignoring Zed, I leaped out of the window. Despite Zed's constant yelling, I grabbed my gun, aimed towards the sky, and pulled the trigger. The bullet went speeding through the air, heading towards a certain figure on the roof. I snapped my fingers and then there was silence. A moment later, Zed's screams could be heard as we landed on the roof. Santa was loading his sleigh and an unconscious Nikola in his bag.

"Did you miss us?" I said.

"Persistent, aren't you?" Santa said.

"Next time warn me before you do that," Zed groaned.

"Complain later. I go high, you go low," I ordered.

Zed and I ran towards the old man as the howling wind blew past us. Santa looked unperturbed as he snapped his fingers. Suddenly, several figures surrounded us. They were moving around us so fast that I couldn't determine who or what they were.

"I hope you don't mind. Dasher, Comet, and Blitzen wanted to see who could take you guys out the fastest," Santa said, chuckling to himself.

We don't have time for these reindeer games.

"Kai," Zed called out.

Zed came charging at me on all fours. Preparing myself, I gave Zed a boost as I tossed him over the circle. While mid-air, Zed changed from a hound to his beast-self and flew towards the old man. Santa smiled in anticipation. Seconds before the two clashed, Santa arched his arm back. Zed pounced, prepared to tackle the enemy.

"Now!" Zed yelled.

Instantly, I switched places with Zed. The sudden swap took Santa by surprise, leaving him stunned long enough for me to score a solid punch to the face. Thanks to Zed's momentum, the punch was enough to send the old man flying back against the chimney.

"That's payback for last time," I declared.

Behind me, the circle of reindeer dispersed and lunged at me. However, Zed grabbed two reindeer by the horns and held them down in place. A shadow then separated from beast-Zed. Zed's human form ran out of the shadow and grabbed onto the remaining reindeer's tail. Even though the two Zeds succeeded in stopping the trio of reindeer from advancing, both Zeds struggled to keep the animals in place.

"Hurry up, Get the girl," The Zed duo growled.

I ran to Nikola and tried to grab her. However, a sudden red beam of light shot out in front of me, cutting off my path. With my advance interrupted, I turned to see where the laser came from. There I saw another reindeer, but not just any reindeer.

"Good job, Rudolph," Santa said, recovering from my assault.

"I was wondering when the most famous reindeer would appear," I said.

I weighed my options. The situation was devolving, and Santa had the upper hand. My thoughts were interrupted by Zed screaming. I saw both Zeds being dragged around in the air, trying desperately to hang on as the reindeer tried to shake them off. Distracted by Zed's cries for help, I felt the heat of a laser heading straight for me. This distraction almost proved fatal. Snapping back, I barely managed to escape by displacing myself towards human-Zed as we flew through the air, hanging on to a reindeer.

"What are you doing?" Zed cried out.

"Saving you," I answered.

Human-Zed had let go of the reindeer's tail, causing us to fall. When Beast-Zed caught wind of our dilemma, he released the other two reindeer and dove to our rescue. Meanwhile, Santa let out a whistle.

"Now Dasher, Dancer, Prancer, and Vixen! On Comet, on Cupid, on Donner, and on Blitzen! Front and center, Rudolph!" Santa called out.

The reindeer gathered in front of Santa's sleigh, preparing to make their grand escape. Thinking fast, I fired a shot at the roof and then displaced all three of us back on solid footing. The two Zeds became one again, as my companion got on all fours in his hound form. Zed gave chase when the sleigh started to take off. Following Zed, I sprinted behind him, trying to catch up. Zed ran ahead while I fired a few shots, hoping to slow down their getaway. However, the roaring winds caused each shot to miss.

We're not gonna make it. My thoughts raced as the sleigh flew off.

Still determined, Zed leaped to grab hold of the departing sleigh. When he missed by just a few inches, he plummeted to the ground. Without a second thought, I jumped off the roof, diving to save Zed. I grabbed hold of him and fired one final shot at Santa Claus.

The bullet barely missed as it whizzed past the old man's head.

"Ha, you missed," Santa said, waving.

However, there was nobody to wave at. Alarmed, Santa turned around to find Beast-Zed ready to wrestle him off his sleigh.

"He wasn't aiming at you," Zed growled.

While my companion kept the old man busy, I made a break for Nikola. Time was of the essence. Despite Beast-Zed's strength, the old man was still superior. Santa grabbed Zed's body and threw him towards me like a projectile, knocking us both off. At the last minute, I threw Vorator, trying to cut the reindeer harness. Unfortunately, my attempt failed as I grazed one of the reindeer instead. With my stamina running on empty, my vision grew hazy as we fell.

"Hang on guys!" a voice rang out.

My eyesight went dark, but I soon felt a warm sensation, followed by something licking my face. I woke up to find Zed and I flying through the air. The both of us were covered in flames.

"What's going on?" Zed panicked.

I remained calm. The flames weren't hot and searing but warm and soothing. My body was relaxed and the heat warmed away any previous exhaustion.

"Phew, I thought I lost you guys," a voice said.

Zed and I looked around to see where the voice came from. In a few seconds, we realized we were flying on a flaming bird.

"Kai, I think we are flying on a flaming chicken," Zed remarked.

"Phoenix actually," the bird said.

"I believe I owe you our thanks Mr. Turner," I said.

Zed's jaw dropped.

"Wait, this flaming chicken is Joe Turner?" Zed asked.

"I'm a Phoenix!" Joe corrected.

Ignoring Joe's protest, Zed continued. "How'd you know Turner was a Phoenix? When did you find out about this?"

"I'll explain later. Right now, I need a status report," I said.

"I saw you guys trying to get on the sleigh and then fall off. I saved you guys from certain death. Now I'm giving chase," Turner explained.

Although it was true, we were giving chase, the gap between us and Santa's sleigh kept growing. Seeing the distance between us expand, I came to a dreadful conclusion.

"We've lost," I said.

"How!?" Zed interjected.

"At this rate, we won't catch up to the sleigh. Remember, we are racing against a guy who delivers presents around the whole world in a day. It's only a matter of time before that old man breaks the sound barrier. We'll never catch him then," I said.

The thought of losing the old man made my blood boil. The distance between us was so far that not even my bullets could help. Suddenly, Zed and I felt a jolt as the flames on Turner grew hotter.

"Hang on tight," Turner said.

Joe flew even faster. There was a spark of hope for a moment, but his efforts still seemed pointless. The distance hadn't closed much. We needed more speed, or at least a way to slow the enemy down.

The frozen winds were blowing against my face as Joe kept trying to close the distance. I took out Vorator, thinking I could do something to displace us forward. That was when I noticed blood on the blade.

"Interesting!" I laughed.

"What's so funny?" Zed asked.

"Has he lost it?" Joe asked.

After regaining my composure, I explained.

"I have an idea, but we need to act fast. At most, I can guarantee five minutes before we lose them. You guys ready?"

Both Zed and Joe nodded in agreement.

"Okay, here's the plan..."

Granted, it was haphazard, but it was our best chance for success.

"Zed, you understand your role, right?" I asked.

"I got it." Zed gave a thumbs up.

I tossed my glove at Zed and he caught it.

"Alright, this is our final assault. We've only got one shot at this," I said.

"Okay, but what are you going to do, Detective?" Joe asked.

"Isn't it obvious?" I chuckled as I stood on the edge of Turner's wing. "I'm the vanguard." That was the last thing

I said before I jumped off.

I was free falling. Then I took a deep breath as the rushing winds nipped at my face. I held tightly to Vorator and I yelled, "FEED!"

Green sparks gathered around the blade and then spread around my whole body. The blood leftover on the blade was slowly being devoured. In seconds, I felt invigorated. Energy was rising throughout my body and adrenaline coursing through my veins. I shot through the sky like a rocket.

"It worked!" I cheered.

I was soaring through the sky like a plane. It took me no time to fly beside Zed and Joe. The former smiled, excited, while the latter stared in utter disbelief.

"I'll fly on ahead, you guys get ready to play your part," I said.

The wind irritated my nose before I flew ahead, I let out a huge sneeze. When I did, a huge laser shot out of my nose. Trying to shake off the sneeze, I noticed my nose turned bright red. A side effect of the transformation.

"Bless you," Zed said.

I waved my hand, thanking Zed before flying off ahead of them. It was amazing being able to zip through the sky at such speeds. I couldn't resist doing a couple of loops in the air. However, as much as I wanted to enjoy the gift of flight, that newfound power was temporary and I had a job to do. The distance to Santa, while great, was easily closed.

He must not have gone light speed yet, I thought.

Approaching the sleigh, I flew side by side with the old man. Whistling to get his attention, Santa looked over at me. The look on his face was so priceless that I winked at him. Santa came to an abrupt stop as I sped ahead. I then stopped in front of the sleigh.

"What's the rush? I didn't even get my gift this year," I said.

"I left your gift down Alderheim's esophagus," Santa said.

"How graphic."

"You persistent little fly. I don't know how you managed to get up here, but let's see how smug you are when I blow you out of the sky," Santa threatened.

"I'm shaking," I mocked.

"Rudolph!" Santa yelled.

On cue, the red-nosed reindeer came charging in. I grabbed Rudolph by the antlers and tried to push back. Even though Rudolph was charging at me, he was still carrying the force of all the other reindeer behind him. To make matters worse, Rudolph's nose gave a menacing glow. Matching his pace, I also focused my energy on my nose as it glowed brightly.

Santa couldn't believe what he was seeing, but it didn't matter.

"Fire!" Santa yelled.

Both Rudolph and I shot our lasers at point-blank range. The force of our beams clashing pushed us back. Our lasers shot back and forth, as Rudolph and I were caught in an intense beam struggle. The sleigh came to a complete halt, which was exactly what I was counting on. During my intense struggle, I snapped my fingers. Suddenly, a figure appeared behind me and jumped off my shoulder. The figure soon split up into three. A trio of Zeds landed on Santa's sleigh.

"You got us by surprise last time," Human-Zed said.

"But let's see you try that again," Beast-Zed growled.

"Bring it," Hound-Zed barked.

"Hurry up," I mumbled.

It was becoming increasingly hard to hold off Rudolph's attacks, and I could feel the effects of Vorator's power surge dwindling. I had a few minutes left at most.

I have to hold out and keep the reindeer busy.

While I fired a laser at the horde, Beast-Zed let loose with a flurry of slashes. With little room to move, Santa protected his vitals. Hound-Zed sunk his teeth in the old man's leg. Santa winced in pain as Beast-Zed tried to capitalize with a swipe to the face. Barely dodging it, Santa swiftly connected with a counter right hook to the face. Beast-Zed staggered back but licked the wound on his cheek. Santa was surprised at the unexpected reaction.

"That was a lot weaker than before," Beast-Zed said and smiled.

Shocked, Santa realized that his right hand was missing his boxing glove. Before the old man could question the sudden disappearance, Beast-Zed wrestled him down. Finally seeing his opportunity, Human-Zed jumped over the scuffle, heading straight for Nikola. Reaching out, Zed managed to grab her by the arm.

Seeing this, Santa uncorked a loud war cry. The sudden cry stunned all the Zeds there. Beast-Zed paused long enough for Santa to headbutt him in the snout, sending Beast-Zed reeling. Santa pulled him back, headbutting him again and again. With his nose broken and blood pouring out, Beast-Zed released his grip. Now freed, the old man knelt down to grab Hound-Zed's by the jaw, forcing it open. Desperate, the bleeding therian tried to grab Santa from behind. Santa only grew angrier, and he gave a sharp elbow to Beast-Zed's gut, sending him to his knees. Once again, Santa tried to rip Hound-Zed in half. Suddenly, a laser came flying, scorching Santa's hat.

Can't have Zed dying again, I thought after I fired a quick shot.

Despite saving Zed, my fight with Rudolph still raged on. Even though I copied the reindeer's powers, his experience made him much more formidable. Rudolph kept firing small shots in quick successive bursts, making evasion almost impossible. I countered each couple of shots with a giant laser of my own. However, the energy it took to charge required more time on my part, something Rudolph enjoyed exploiting during our mid-air combat. When Rudolph chased me around firing, I threw my knife at point-blank range.

The reindeer avoided my knife as I displaced myself behind him and fired a couple of shots with Scarlet Hiro. Typically, my bullets would be no match for a laser. But my aim was to force Rudolph to move. Avoiding my bullets, Rudolph returned fire but was surprised by my sudden disappearance. Above, I gathered as much energy as I could. Sensing danger, Rudolph looked up just in time to see a laser coming down on his head. Rudolph quickly reacted with a giant laser of his own, though it was no match for mine. Rudolph was being pushed down to earth.

I'm winning.

My victory didn't last long. As our beam struggle continued, I felt the energy from my laser becoming weaker and more unstable while Rudolph's grew stronger and more focused. Rudolph was rising up as I slowly felt myself sinking. My red nose started to flicker.

Time's up.

Suddenly, my beautiful gift of flight was blasted out of the sky by the opposing laser. I barely managed to avoid the worst of the blast, but my arm and leg suffered severe burns.

"Kai!" Zed yelled.

I plummeted to the ground while Zed stared in horror.

Seeing the opportunity, the sly old man grabbed the two Zeds and threw them overboard, knocking over the third Zed in the process. I tried displacing myself to Zed's side, but every time I tried, green sparks fizzled out. I was out of mana, out of options, and out of hope. As I was approaching the ground, my vision faded to black. The last thing I remembered hearing was Santa's jolly laughter.

answered.

"That may be a problem," Kai said.

"How? Elizabeth might be troublesome as a Beastman, but she didn't strike me as the violent type," I said.

"Elizabeth is the least of our concerns. Mary is who I'm worried about," Kai corrected.

"The doll?" I asked.

"I'll explain later. Right now, we need to find Zed," Kai said as he hurried past me.

"How do you expect to find him in this giant manor?" I asked.

"Normally, I would appear before him, but I can't afford to waste the mana bringing us both," Kai mumbled.

"What?"

"Don't worry, I can hear him. Follow me," Kai said as he pointed to his ears.

"Aren't you forgetting something?" I asked.

Kai arched an eyebrow. I was going to return his gun, but then the gun vanished from my hand. Kai was already twirling around his gun without care.

"You okay, Mr. Turner? You look like you've lost something," Kai said.

He set me up.

"You coming?" he asked.

At that point, any further argument would be pointless. I just followed. As we made our way to god knows where, Kai filled me in about Mary the doll. Her Grace was called Shadow Theater and it was a problematic ability.

"You think both maids are in on this scheme?" I asked.

"Their disappearance while things went crazy is too suspicious to ignore. I'm certain at least one of them is involved," he said.

"And you're more suspicious of the doll?" I mocked.

"That doll has the ability to control people, and we know neither the limit nor the range of her Grace. For all we know, she could control hundreds of people or things from miles away," Kai argued.

"When you put it that way, how do we counter it?" I asked.

"Got a light?" Kai asked. I didn't understand the question, so Kai continued, "At the end of the day she needs the shadows to control her target, so-"

Kai suddenly stopped mid-sentence as he stared at the wall before us.

"Move!" Kai yelled.

We both jumped out of the way as something came crashing through the wall. A body came flying in. Kai sped off to inspect it and I followed behind to catch a glimpse. I didn't recognize the person. As a matter of fact, the face looked like it was caved in, making it completely unrecognizable. Whoever they were, they must've died instantly. The detective stood motionless above the body. Before I could ask him what was wrong, I felt a sharp chill in my spine. Kai's face changed.

I didn't think he could look so upset. The mood shifted. Suddenly, the deceased body in front of us turned black and then it melted into the ground. It dissolved into a black stain. The surrounding mood had lightened up.

"Well, I think I know where Zed is," Kai said, relieved.

"Where?" I asked.

The black stain on the ground came alive as it slunk past us, returning through the hole in the wall.

"Follow the shadow," Kai pointed.

The detective and I peeked through the hole. The body had

come through a series of walls. Through the hole, we could see a hulking figure and Elizabeth ganging up on a dog.

"If I was a betting man, I'd say that hulking figure is Santa Claus and he's about to make mincemeat of your pal, Zed."

"Correct. We're just in time."

"Alright, let's get this over with," I said.

I was ready to spring into action, but Kai grabbed me by the shoulder.

"Hold on, we still don't know what we are jumping into," Kai said.

"Are you suggesting we just watch?" I asked.

"I'm saying we can't blindly rush in. I picked a fight with that old man and it nearly cost me. Nikola is still there, so we can't risk an all-out fight if it means more casualties."

"Any suggestions?"

Once again, that smile crept onto his face.

"Divide and conquer," Kai said.

I raised my eyebrow as he continued.

"I'll pop over there and scope out the situation. If both the maids are involved, Zed and I will try to split up our assailants, giving you a chance to incapacitate the doll," Kai explained.

"Good enough," I said.

Snapping his fingers, Kai vanished.

"How does he do that?" I mumbled.

The plan went off without a hitch. I overheard Kai and Zed mention that Elizabeth was possessed while they fought. Sticking to the plan, the two investigators made their escape, prompting Santa and Elizabeth to pursue them. That's when I arrived at the scene. The area those four left behind looked as if a tornado had wrecked the place. There was nothing left except a broken couch, pieces of rubble, and excessive claw marks.

I don't even know where to look, I thought.

I tried inspecting the floor, hoping for footprints. Instead, I found traces of weird black lines on the ground. On one end, the lines led toward where Kai and his partner ran off. On the other end, the lines led around the corner. I followed the latter and arrived at a room filled with snow globes. The further ahead I walked, the more I heard the faint sound of music. It grew louder the deeper I traversed. The song sounded like it was coming from a music box. When I finally made it to the center of the room, I was greeted by the second maid putting on quite a show.

Mary was performing an exquisite dance routine to the music. It didn't seem like she noticed me until I gave her a round of applause. The doll turned her head to stare at me, but her body kept dancing without missing a beat.

"That's a pretty nice performance you got there. Any chance you can take a pause for the cause?" I said as I approached.

The doll continued to dance.

"The hard way it is," I said, moving towards the doll.

A layer of glass stopped my advance. The doll was hiding behind the glass to prevent any interruptions. I knocked on the glass a few times. By the density, I suspected it was both bulletproof and shatterproof.

Guess I can't use brute force to get in.

My options were limited and only one idea came to my mind. I took off my vest, shirt, tie, and pants. Taking out a cigar from my pocket, I took another glance at Mary.

"I have a question," I said to the dancing doll. I put the cigar in my mouth and grinned. "Got a light?"

Chapter XXI

My cigar lit up and I took a few puffs. Fire suddenly surrounded my feet. My body ignited next, and I was completely engulfed in flames. Then the entire room lit up like a giant furnace. Still, the doll continued to dance. I gazed over the lines of shadows. They were dwindling slightly, but remained prominent.

"Guess I'll turn it up," I declared.

Understood.

The flames grew larger and hotter. Still, the stupid doll ignored me. Taking a deep breath, I increased the output. The flames had engulfed the entire room. The flames had engulfed the entire room. Suddenly, a series of snow globes began exploding at random. The doll finally turned her head.

"Finally paying attention, huh?" I said.

Flames continued to pour out of me as I stared at the glass wall separating us. I felt the flames behind me grow and morph into wings. I caught a brief glimpse of my silhouette on the glass. The wings wrapped around me, covering me in their warm embrace, and then they extended wide, filling the room with fire. The glass separating us finally cracked. Mary slowly moved her feet back. Smiling, I walked forward and put my hand on the glass. The doll shook uncontrollably as I melted the glass before it's eyes.

"First time I've ever seen a doll experience fear," I said.

The flames roared behind me as I slowly reached out to grab Mary. The doll made a break for it, trying to avoid the sea of flames. I watched casually as Mary, covered in scorch marks, ran away. With a flap of my wings, I sped off, closing the distance between us.

"Burn," I said as a wall of flame erupted from the ground, cutting off the doll's escape route.

Trapped like a rat, Mary shook violently. There was no room for escape. Landing in front of her, I raised my hand, preparing to incinerate the puppet master.

"Any last words?" I said.

Suddenly, the doll's eyes rolled back and it collapsed. Realizing that Mary was down for the count, my flames died down as I knelt beside her. I picked up the lifeless doll and shook it.

"You weren't so tough," I said.

Then I felt a mysterious force pulling me in. More accurately, the force was pulling Mary, trying to pry the doll from my fingers.

"What the hell?"

I tried to reinforce my grip, but the force tried to pull me in as well. Eventually, Mary was yanked out of my hand and flew down the corridor. I was about to give chase until I felt a cool breeze blow past.

"I should probably put some clothes on."

After taking a minute to dress myself, I ran down the corridor.

"Damn it!" a voice yelled.

I saw the investigative duo looking worse for wear. After being greeted with a gun to my face, again, the three of us exchanged information. I brought Kai up to speed on what happened to our 'guest' and the detective desperately tried to weigh his options.

"Zed, how are you feeling?" Kai asked.

"Not quite one hundred percent, but good enough," Zed answered.

"Good. Turner, you hold down the fort in case we need backup," Kai ordered.

"Fine. What are you going to do?" I asked.

Kai simply smiled at the question. After some brief banter between Kai and Zed, I was tempted to ignore the two idiots. I expected that they had some backup plan, but what happened next was a shocker. The mad detective threw himself and his partner out of a window. A gunshot followed and I raced to the window. But when I looked outside, I saw nothing but snow. I figured Kai must've used his Grace.

"Would've been nice if I knew where they went," I said.

After waiting for a while, I was getting bored. I wasn't sure what I was waiting for. Suddenly, I heard an explosion coming from overhead.

The roof?

I turned to the window and saw a pack of flying reindeer trying to shake Kai and Zed off.

"What's he doing?" I asked.

Watching the mid-air rodeo put me in the mood for another cigar. However, before I lit one, the duo fell off the sleigh.

I suppose this counts as backup, I thought.

Jumping out of the window, my body ignited. The flames roared as they enveloped my body. My clothes incinerated as my body grew. My arms morphed into flaming wings. As I beat them, the heat coming from them melted the snow beneath me. With each flap of my wings, I soared higher into the sky, catching the gumshoe and his companion with ease.

"Phew, I thought I lost you guys," I sighed in relief.

"Kai, I think we are flying on a flaming chicken," that little mutt said.

"Phoenix, actually," I corrected.

"I see." The detective took a moment to look around. "I believe I owe you our thanks, Mr. Turner," Kai said.

We took a moment to bring each other up to speed on the situation. Eventually, Kai explained that catching up to Santa Claus was near impossible as the sleigh kept gaining speed.

"Hang on tight," I yelled.

I wasn't ready to give up yet, so I tried to gain more speed. Which was easier said than done. The problem was my passengers. The faster I move, the higher my overall body temperature rises. This made it very difficult for me to pick up enough speed without burning those two alive. As I attempted this feat, the sound of obnoxious laughter interrupted me.

"I see," the detective said.

Zed and I questioned Kai's sanity, but there was a renewed sense of determination in his voice.

"Guys, I have a plan, but we need to act fast. At most I can guarantee five minutes before Santa escapes. You guys in?" Kai asked.

Zed and I both nodded. Truth be told, I was curious about what this gumshoe could come up with in the seemingly hopeless situation.

"Okay, so here's the plan. We need to remind ourselves that this isn't a war of attrition. This is a game of keep away," Kai explained.

"Meaning?" I asked.

"He means we don't have to win. We just need to make sure Santa loses by stealing Nikola away from him," Zed answered.

"And thanks to this," Kai revealed his knife, "I have a way to fast travel over to that sleigh, but that's the easy part. The problem is that Santa won't let me get near Nikola since that old man has an idea of how my Grace works. That's where Zed comes in. I'll give Zed one of my gloves with a rune on it. All you need to do is put a hand on Nikola's body."

"And then what?" I asked.

"Then Kai will handle the rest," Zed said.

"Remember, Zed, you need to be in your human form to use my glove. The glove won't fit on your other forms. Zed, you understand your role?" Kai asked.

"I got it," Zed replied.

"Meanwhile, I'll try to slow down the sleigh enough to give Mr. Turner a chance to catch up and Zed a chance to complete his job. Mr. Turner, your job is to catch us if the plan goes awry," Kai explained.

"So just keep doing what I've been doing," I said.

"Alright guys, this is our final assault. We only get one shot, so we can't fail," Kai said.

"Okay, but how do you plan on slowing down the sleigh?" I asked.

After chuckling to himself, Kai said, "By being the vanguard."

After those final words, the mad detective fell off.

"Has he lost it!" I yelled.

"Relax, just give him a minute," Zed reassured.

I found it unnerving how calm Zed sounded as his partner was free falling. Seconds later, something blasted through the air like a missile. I was left speechless when I saw the flying projectile was Kai flying side by side, waving at me.

"I'll fly ahead, you guys get ready to move," Kai said as he sped off. However, his ascent was cut short when the man let out a terrifying sneeze, shooting out a laser.

What is he? I thought.

After a quick, "Bless you," from Zed. Kai flew ahead

"Told you he needed a minute," Zed affirmed.

It didn't take long for Kai to make contact. Just like he said, Kai made the sleigh come to a complete halt.

"Look alive, Joe! My turn should be next," Zed affirmed.

Before I could respond, an explosion of lasers clashed, causing a bizarre light show.

"That's one hell of a distraction," I said.

My comment fell on deaf ears as Zed disappeared from my back. I figured it was due to Kai's "fast travel," and this sudden disappearance worked in my favor.

Now nothing is holding me back, I thought.

I blazed forward like a jet quickly picking up speed. Meanwhile, Kai and another reindeer were engaged in a brutal dog fight. It was easy to see who had the advantage between the two. Kai was out of his depth, but he still managed to hold his own. I kept gaining speed, closing the gap between me and the sleigh. Unfortunately, after one final clash between those mid-air titans, Kai was blasted out of the sky. A trio of Zeds quickly followed, plummeting to their doom.

Damn it!

Focusing my flames on the edge of my wings, I propelled myself even faster. Meanwhile, two of the Zeds grabbed the third and performed a mid-air throw aimed at Kai.

"Gotcha!" Zed said.

Zed grabbed hold of Kai. Then the other two forms dispersed and then reappeared around Kai. I didn't quite understand what Zed was up to until I saw each form linking their arms together.

"Joe!" Zed yelled out, reaching a hand towards me.

He's forming a ladder, I realized as I finally grabbed his hand with my talon.

I made an emergency landing lest I burned my passengers alive. Grounded, we got a good glimpse of Santa flying away.

"Merry Christmas," the man yelled out.

Even though I didn't have any personal stakes in the battle, it still felt annoying to face our failure. I turned to see how the other two were handling the situation. Instead, I saw Zed on all fours licking Kai's face continuously.

"Wake up! Come on, wake up!" Zed said furiously.

The detective's arms and legs were in bad shape.

"Allow me," I said.

I moved Zed aside to inspect Kai's wounds then conjured up some phoenix fire in my hand and waved it over his injuries.

"What are you doing?" Zed asked.

"Healing him, the fire should help neutralize the pain."

"That's nice and all, but why are you naked?" Zed asked.

Before I could answer, Kai's eyes shot open. At first, he looked relieved as he saw us. However, that look morphed into confusion.

"Why are you naked?" Kai asked.

"Long story," I said.

"I don't think I want to know either. Can someone bring me up to speed?" Kai asked.

I explained to Kai about our apparent defeat. Surprisingly, the detective didn't look bothered.

"Zed," Kai called out. "Did you get it done?"

"Of course. That old fart is probably up there laughing and

thinking he's won," Zed said while returning Kai's glove.

"Excellent," Kai smiled.

Kai then took out a hand-sized box and fiddled around with it. I had no idea what he was up to, but it involved a boxing glove. Regardless, when Kai finished, the box had weird markings on it. Kai gave the box a quick wind-up. Afterwards, he took out a handkerchief and placed it over the box.

"Gentlemen, now you see it," Kai snapped his fingers as he uncovered the box. "Now you don't."

The box was gone. I wasn't the least bit impressed. But, before I replied, Nikola Evergreen appeared in his arms.

"How the hell did you do that?" I asked.

"That's an even longer story," Kai winked. "Right now, I need one of you to hold the girl, preferably not the streaker."

Zed stood on his two legs and took Nikola off Kai's hands. Afterwards, Kai immediately collapsed.

"Is he still hurt?" I asked.

"No, he's just tired. Let him rest," Zed said.

Looking at the detective, it was clear that he was fast asleep. I had mixed opinions about the guy, but I had to admit he was right about one thing.

"This was one hell of a story."

Chapter XXII

That was an exhausting night. I figured following up on that letter would lead us to something interesting, but I hadn't expected a rumble with Santa Claus. There's never a dull moment with Kai.

After we returned to Evergreen Manor, we followed Kai's lead and got some rest. Joe needed to find some clothes while I was carrying Nikola back to her room. With that done, I still wasn't convinced we were out of the woods yet. I got down on all fours and stayed in the corner of the room to keep watch. I fell asleep as soon as I hit the ground. Hours later, I felt the sun peek through the blinds.

"Few more minutes," I said as I covered my eyes.

Sadly, those few minutes were cut short by a sudden shriek. My ears perked up as I stood up.

"Where am I? How'd I get here? Was that all a dream?" Nikola spat out a volley of questions in her confused state.

"I assure you, last night was no dream," I said.

Nikola spun around, clearly unhappy to see me in her room. I was too groggy to care.

"I carried you here," I explained.

My explanations did nothing to calm her down and she kept inching towards the door.

It's too early for me to chase you around, I thought.

"Tell me what happened," she asked.

Surprisingly, instead of running away, Nikola dug for answers. I explained everything that happened after Kai shot her. Her face had a mix of complicated emotions as I explained.

"And with a snap of his fingers, Kai got you back relatively safe and sound," I finished.

Nikola looked downcast, "So he just left?" she asked. "My father, my real father, just left? Just like that? Without noticing I disappeared?"

It was sad, but I didn't have an answer for her.

"You can't answer," she said with trembling hands.

Then her somber mood disappeared as quickly as it came.

"Oh well. It can't be helped. If I really want an answer I should ask that 'great detective,'" Nikola said, condescendingly. "Where is he? There's still some unfinished business to discuss."

In an instant, Kai appeared behind me.

"Morning, sleeping beauty," he said.

I've grown used to Kai's antics for the most part, but his sudden appearance was a shock for Nikola, who scrambled backwards when she saw him.

Regaining her composure, Nikola said, "It's my understanding that you shot me?"

"Yeah, pretty much," Kai answered.

"Why'd you do that?!" Nikola yelled.

Kai arched an eyebrow at Nikola.

"You must be either very brave or very stupid to yell at the guy that shot you. Who's to say I won't do it again?" Kai said.

The air grew cold and Nikola's brow tensed up for a moment.

"Shut up," Nikola shot back. "If you really intended to kill me, you could've just finished the job while I was unconscious."

"You got me there," Kai shrugged.

"Then why?" Nikola asked.

"I needed to prove that your father, Santa Claus, is both real and the culprit. I needed to draw him out, so I used his only daughter as bait," Kai explained.

"And what if you were wrong? I could've died for nothing," she countered.

"Either way, your plan would've gone up in smoke," Kai said.

You're full of it, I snorted.

Kai and I both knew he would have displaced the bullet before it ever touched her.

"You make it sound like you've won. But your partner just explained that Santa managed to escape. You still have no proof," Nikola explained.

"Must be killing you that your dad left you behind," Kai said.

"Who cares? I already got what I needed," Nikola said.

You're also full of it, I thought.

I could already smell her fear, but then I noticed Nikola's hand tremble—something I'm certain Kai also noticed.

"Unfortunately, your comment about not having proof no longer applies," Kai said.

Nikola was silent as Kai handed her a piece of paper. Her eyes widened as she read.

"What is this?" she asked.

"A paternity test. Your dad and I got into a bit of a scuffle. While we fought, I managed to get a few hairs off him. It may not be enough to prove he is Santa Claus, but it is enough to prove someone related to you is responsible for all of this. Most importantly, it proves you're not the daughter of

Alderhiem Evergreen," Kai explained.

For a moment, Nikola looked unsure as she held the test results. Feigning indifference, Nikola tossed the paper aside.

"Not bad, detective, but so what? There still is Evergreen's will. Even with that evidence,

Evergreen doesn't have a sole heir. If he decided to leave everything to me, it could still hold up in court."

"Not if it's a fake," I countered.

"With what proof?" she retorted.

Kai shook his head slowly and mumbled, "An actress to the end."

"What?" Nikola said.

"I admire your tenacity, but since you're determined to play this role, I'll have to play mine."

Nikola arched an eyebrow.

"There's something else I need to show you," Kai said, revealing a blank piece of paper.

"What's that supposed to be?" Nikola asked.

"This I found inside Evergreen's desk. It was hidden in a secret compartment. Santa must've missed it. I wasn't sure what it was, but after last night, a thought came to mind." Kai took out a lighter and continued, "Evergreen clearly anticipated his death, so he must've prepared everything in advance," Kai said as he gently hovered the paper over the flame.

After a moment, words started to become visible.

"As you can see, this is Evergreen's last will and testament. The will reveals that Evergreen wanted his estate to be given to charity. It reveals your mother's scandal and explains that you were never his actual daughter. Evergreen was willing to spite you even in death. Of course, it will take some lawyers and authenticators to prove that this was written by Alderheim. However, by the look on your face, you already know the truth," Kai explained.

Nikola was too stunned to speak.

"In other words," Kai continued, "you lose."

"Lose?" Nikola mumbled.

"With these pieces of evidence, you'll be completely blocked off from the Evergreen fortune. You may not be charged as an accessory to murder, but when this comes out, you'll be left with nothing. Although, I wonder if that's what you really care about," Kai explained.

Nikola remained silent.

"There's something I'd like to show you," Kai said as he extended a hand to her.

Nikola stared at his hand while gripping the hem of her dress. She took a step back.

"You said it yourself, if I wanted you dead I would've done it already," Kai reassured.

Nikola halted, staring up at Kai as he smiled. After a moment, he said.

"I told you something interesting would happen, didn't I?"

Chapter XXIII

Honestly, I was surprised when she took my hand. I was the man who was about to leave her with nothing. The thought didn't linger for very long. Instead, I displaced the three of us to a remote location outside. It was cold, but not freezing. Snow was on the ground around us as we stood on the top of the hill. The sun shined beautifully. While Zed went off to play in the snow, Nikola and I watched silently.

"So, why did you take me here?" Nikola eventually asked.

"I thought this would be a good place to catch the sunrise," I answered.

"You don't strike me as the romantic type," Nikola countered.

"That's because you never got to know me," I said.

"Is this a joke to you?"

"If it is, I'm wondering what the punchline is."

"Enough, you win. Is that what you want to hear? Is this just some kind of victory lap for you?"

I remained silent as Nikola continued.

"The great detective figured it all out. You revealed the true scandal behind the Evergreen family. You discovered my true origins and my real father. Then you managed to force my father to leave me behind and discovered Alderheim's will.

Congratulations. Not only have you beaten me, you've left me with nothing. No, you've left me with less than nothing. You must be so proud!" Nikola yelled.

Zed overheard us and looked in our direction. Nikola's hands were shaking and her eyes grew moist.

"That's where you're wrong," I said. "I wasn't able to figure out how you and the old man found each other. It's been bothering me."

"You brought me out here just for that?" Nikola questioned.

"Color me curious, how did you find out that Santa Claus was your real father?"

Irritated, Nikola reluctantly answered me, "I wrote the confiscated letters weeks ago. By late November, people were preparing for the Christmas holiday. Despite having a strict father, I was also preparing for the holiday. There was always something about this time of year that made me feel alive. Looking back, that was probably something I inherited from my father," Nikola paused.

For a moment, she looked to the sky. Zed, now interested in her story, came closer. Nikola continued,

"I was shopping at the mall. I may not have been his daughter, but I was still given an allowance. Enough to buy a store or two."

Must be nice, I thought as I tried to hide my disdain.

Nikola continued, "At the center of the mall was a huge Christmas tree. It was beautiful with lights dancing around the tree. A mall Santa was there. I assumed it was just another guy in a suit. But something was different this time. He felt so familiar, and when he turned to look at me, I could see that he felt the same way. I didn't know why, but we were drawn to each other," Nikola explained.

Familial resonance?

"We got to talking. He must've known who I was. We talked about my mother. He talked about her as if he knew her. I mean, really knew her, better than my stepfather. It didn't take me long to learn the truth, all the signs were there. When we spoke, I felt accepted, not tolerated. Not some sort of prize, celebrity, trust-fund baby, or even a painful reminder. I felt-"

"Loved," I finished.

Nikola bit her lip as she looked down.

"Eventually, I confronted him and asked why he never came for me. He claimed he didn't know, but swore he would try to make up for lost time, starting by freeing me from Evergreen."

"And so the plot to kill Evergreen was conceived," Zed commented.

"That was the plan. Then you two got involved," Nikola said as she stared at me with those fiery blue eyes. "You couldn't just leave this alone. That letter was supposed to serve as a warning. Instead, you took it as a challenge. Now everything is ruined. My mother is dead. The man I knew as my father is dead. My real father left me behind, and I don't know if I'll ever see him again. I've been stripped of any claim to an inheritance. And it's all your fault! I'm . . . I'm..." she stammered.

Nikola's fist shook as she faced me. Zed growled, but I raised a hand to silence him.

"I'm not an Evergreen. I'm barely a Claus. I'm all alone now," Nikola admitted as the tears streamed down her face.

"You're right," I said. "You're not an Evergreen, and being a Claus may not be an option. But I believe you're forgetting something important."

"What?" Nikola said.

Even Zed looked puzzled, not sure what I was referring to.

"Which reminds me," I said, "it was pretty diabolical how Evergreen forced Maria into marriage. It was either marry the megalomaniac or have her family suffer from financial ruin."

"Get to your point," Nikola said.

"How did Evergreen gain such control over the Swan's finances?"

I asked.

Nikola stared daggers at me, clearly frustrated.

"What does it matter? What's the point in asking that now?" Nikola said.

"My point is," I said and then cleared my throat. "You haven't lost everything! You're stuck between an Evergreen and a Claus. But who cares about that when you're a Swan?"

Surprised by my declaration, Nikola was speechless.

"You're the spitting image of your mother, right down to the eyes. I've seen you dance and I've seen your performance throughout this case. It was nothing short of stellar," I said.

Albeit annoying.

"You think an Evergreen or a Claus could've done that? No, only a Swan could've pulled off such a performance."

"What does it matter if I'm the only Swan left?" she asked.

"About that," I said.

I took out the folder I found in Evergreen's desk and revealed the second blank piece of paper.

"I was curious how Evergreen was able to blackmail your mother, so I did some digging."

I took out my lighter, and just like before, I hovered the paper over the flame.

"Somehow, Evergreen managed to acquire the rights to the land the Swan family was living on. I'm not sure if he stole the rights, bought it, or tricked the Swans into giving it to him," I continued.

The words on the page began to appear.

"As you can see, there is deed to the estate, including the Swan theater. Seeing as you're a Swan, it's only right that you inherit your true birthright," I explained as I handed Nikola the document.

I was hoping she'd be a little relieved, but I suppose that was too much to ask for at that moment. Nikola just looked at the document and blinked.

"What do you expect me to do with this?" She asked.

"Whatever you want," I answered.

Reluctantly, Nikola accepted the paper and stared at it blankly. I could read the thoughts running through her mind as she struggled with her decision.

"By the way," I said. "If you need help deciding what to do, I have a suggestion."

"So there is a catch," Nikola said, dejected.

"Just hear me out. While you were out, I asked Woodrow to help me look into something. The butler had intimate knowledge of Evergreen's shady dealings. As it turns out, after Maria died, Evergreen removed the Swan family from the land. However, with Woodrow's help, we were able to track them down," I explained.

"My grandparents are alive?"

"Yes. And I can't imagine it was easy for them to migrate to a whole new location with their lives uprooted," I added.

"Where are they?" she asked.

I walked to the edge of the hill and pointed to a long cabin below. It was a modest home with a large stack of firewood beside it. Smoke rose from the chimney. Nikola looked down and took a single step back.

"This is a joke, right?" Nikola asked.

"No joke," I said.

"But why? Why do all this for me?" Nikola asked.

"Call it a hunch," I said.

"What?" Nikola asked.

"Which is the real Nikola? The cold woman that willingly participated in her stepfather's murder for money and power or the girl that felt oppressed by living her whole life under the thumb of a megalomaniac? I'm choosing to believe the latter and giving you a new lease on life. However, I warn you," my voice turned cold, "this is a once-in-a-lifetime opportunity. If I find out you're plotting murders again, I'll lock you up in a cage myself."

"Is that a promise?" Nikola asked tenderly.

I nodded. "If not, I can take you into custody right now." My hand hovered, ready to snap my fingers.

Nikola's features softened as she shook her head. I lowered my hand and reached for her.

"Ready to find out who you are?" I asked.

Nikola stared at my hand, conflicted. Her hand reached for mine, still hesitant. After a deep breath, Nikola gathered her resolve and took my hand.

Standing at the front door, Nikola stared in anticipation. The door was well-crafted, as was the rest of the cabin. A swan was carved in the center of the door.

How fancy, I thought.

Nikola stood next to me, shaking continuously.

"You cold?" I asked.

"Yes. No, er, I don't know," she said. "I've never met my grandparents before. My mom hardly ever mentioned them. I'm just not sure what to expect," Nikola explained as she wrapped her arms around herself.

"It doesn't matter," I said.

Surprised, the young Swan stared at me.

"What matters is how we pick ourselves up, and for a star," I said as I tapped her forehead.

The sudden tap caused Nikola to close her eyes. As she opened them, Nikola found herself alone. She looked around frantically, only to realize I was nowhere to be found. It was just her and the door behind her.

"We expect nothing less than to get back up in style," she said.

Turning to face the door to her new life, after a deep breath, Nikola knocked on the door.

I returned to the top of the hill with Zed. With a bird's eye view, I was able to see the young Swan open the doors to a new start and then I turned away.

"Leaving so soon? After sharing such a tender moment, I figured you'd meet the rest of the family," Zed teased.

"You enjoyed the view from up here?" I said.

Zed gave an innocent smile as we walked.

"In all seriousness, you think this is a good idea?" Zed asked.

"Hopefully, but what happens next is up to her. I'm just giving a friendly nudge," I answered.

"That's not what I meant. Santa Claus is still out there. He could still try to steal Nikola away again."

"Doubtful. He left DNA at the crime scene and his description has been given to the authorities. Santa is a wanted man. He won't be able to come and go as he pleases. Plus, if he really loves his daughter, he'll realize that her being with her other family is better than being with a fugitive," I explained.

"I have one more question. What did you replace Nikola

with on the sleigh?"

I yawned, then gave a sly grin.

"I just returned something I borrowed."

Interlude III

Hours earlier.

A boisterous laugh echoed in the twilight. Santa Claus was reveling in his victory and escape from his enemies. Then he heard something. Music. The sound of the tune was coming from his bag of presents.

Turning around, Santa first noticed that Nikola had vanished. Before he could process this, the music grew louder and louder. Annoyed, the man rummaged through his bag, looking for the source of the music. He found the music box and noticed the words etched on it. Taking out his glasses to read the words, the music came to an end. Before Santa could finish reading, a boxing glove sprang out of the box. The glove slammed into his face, sending him flying off his sleigh.

On the box were the words, *Don't open till Xmas -Kai.*

Epilogue

After giving our statements to the authorities, it was revealed that Kai was right about the evidence against Nikola. It was circumstantial at best. Her supposed involvement was hidden pretty well, all things considered. Of course, Woodrow being unwilling to testify against her helped. As far as the world was concerned, Nikola was an innocent victim. Revealing Santa Claus as the culprit was easier than expected. Of course, we couldn't directly call him by name lest we became a laughingstock. We gave our description and it matched an individual who had been involved in a couple of breaking and entering cases. The cops pegged this case as a robbery gone wrong.

The Evergreen estate was supposed to be donated, but an article in the EMW described that all of the Evergreen assets had been seized. Alderheim's shady business dealings, blackmail, and abuses were made public. The article also revealed the paper trail to offshore accounts, along with a certain black book that exposed a list of business partners who were complicit in those deals, including something with a strange G symbol in the center of it. This ruffled enough feathers to warrant a full-scale investigation. However, they have yet to find a paper trail revealing what this Livecorp was. The investigation is currently still ongoing. The author of the article goes by the pseudonym Flamehawk. Personally, I think

'Flaming Chicken' is a better name.

Woodrow cooperated with law enforcement during the investigation. Surprisingly, he served no prison time. We suspected he cut some kind of deal. Afterwards, he mentioned something about going to work for the Swan family. Apparently, it had something to do with repaying a debt. Elizabeth also decided to work for the Swan family. Strangely, the goat maid had no recollection of what happened while she was possessed. All she remembered was that she was preparing coffee and then she suddenly blacked out. By the time she regained consciousness, she was in the middle of the hallway with her clothes tattered and her body sore from an intense workout. No one seems to know what became of Mary. The doll maid seemed to have completely disappeared. Not sure if that's a cause for concern yet. As for Kai and I...

Months later

"There's nothing good to watch," I said, lazily flipping through the TV channels.

"If you're going to watch TV, please pick a channel and watch," Kai said, reading the newspaper.

I stopped on an interview. It wasn't a big deal at first, but then Kai and I heard a familiar voice on TV. Putting the newspaper down, Kai turned his attention to the screen. There was Nikola with a bright smile.

"Be sure to catch the thrilling installment of the Swan Princess performed by lead actress Nikola Swan. Critics rate it 4.5 out of 5. Catch it live, only in the Swan Theater,"

As the interview came to an end, I saw a brief smile on Kai's face.

"Aww how cute. Should I buy our tickets now?" I teased.

"Not interested," Kai said, returning his attention to the

paper.

"Oh, so you weren't smiling?"

"No idea what you're talking about."

Before I could tease him further, the phone suddenly rang.

"Cypher Inc., where we decipher your problems with a snap. How may we be of service?" Kai quickly answered.

I couldn't exactly hear what was being said on the other side. From Kai's face, I already surmised what the call was about. After writing down an address, Kai leaned back in his chair. And with his signature smile, Kai said, "How interesting. So what's the case?"

The End?

Acknowledgments

Hello everyone, Mister X here. I would like to give you, dear reader, a sincere thank you for reading my book in its entirety. Around the holidays, Santa is usually a hero who saves the day. So this time I thought, why not make him a villain? This work was initially a short story, but I enjoyed the concept so much that I turned it into a book. I hope I have kept you captivated from start to finish and that you have enjoyed Cypher Inc.'s adventure as much as I have. There were many challenges in making this book, so I'd like to thank all the people special to me who helped me bring this book to life. Finally, I'd like to thank the rest of my friends for keeping it real and making this book the best it can be. There are more stories and adventures on the way! So please follow me on Instagram @extraordinarymisterx for updates. Thank you again for reading.

Kai and Zed will return!

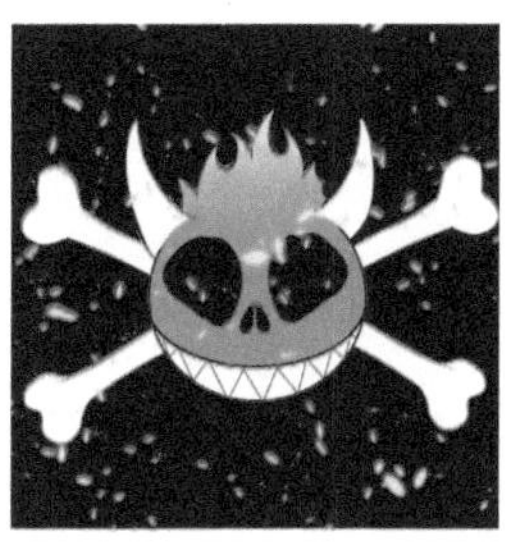

About the Author

Mister X is a first-time novelist and long-time savant of the mystery genre. He has spent long hours studying the art of deduction and perfecting his problem-solving skills. When X is not writing or solving the world's mysteries, you can find him exploring other worlds through the window of the book or a video game. He also enjoys mixed martial arts training, Dungeons and Dragons, and tending to his plants.

You can connect with me on:

https://www.facebook.com/profile.php?id=61569979792089

https://www.instagram.com/extraordinarymisterx